DEAD RECKONING

AN AL PENNYBACK MYSTERY

CHARLES RAY

U2S hurd press

North Potomac, MD

Cover photograph by author

Printed in the United States of America.

ISBN: 0692747575
ISBN-13: 978-0692747575

Dedication

To my readers. You are why I do this. You, the reader, are why any writer sits down day after day, pounding out word after word, page after page. I hope you will find something to like about this book, and if you do, that you'll take the time to write a review—no matter how short—because, reviews draw attention to books, attract new readers, and that's what we writers are all about, getting more people to read what we write.

Also to my wonderful grandchildren, Sammie, Catie, and Tommy.

Chapter
One

March 15, 2003, Garrett County, Western Maryland

A low-hanging tree branch hit me in the face. It hurt like hell, but was nothing compared to the burning pain in my left thigh. The wound, caused by a 9mm through and through, was no longer bleeding thanks to my remembering an old folk remedy my grandmother taught me when I was growing up in East Texas. A poultice of mud—I shuddered at the thought of the nasty bugs probably growing in it—and oak leaves staunched the blood flow. But, it still felt like someone had jammed a hot poker into my leg and left it there.

My breath came in ragged gasps, and my lungs were on fire. To add to the catalogue of problems, my vision was blurred. I stopped my limping run and leaned my forehead against the rough gray bark of a tree, sucking air into my oxygen-starved lungs in large gulps.

I wanted to sit down—no, lie down—and rest. I couldn't. If I didn't stay on my feet, they'd catch me. If I lay down, I would never get back up. I wasn't ready for the big sleep.

And, I'd be damned if I'd let the big guy and his thugs get me. That smug Russian bastard thought he was hot shit. Well, I planned to show him. I'd laugh in his ugly Slavic face as I kicked his nuts up to his Adam's apple.

And, right after that, I'd whip my cape back and fly off to my fortress of solitude.

Who the hell was I kidding? I was as good as dead.

I turned slowly and rested with my back against the tree. Looking up, I could only see slivers of the bright blue sky through the leaves of the towering trees, mostly giant hemlocks, covering the steep hill I'd been climbing for what felt like weeks, although I knew it had only been an hour since I decided that up was the safest way to go to elude my pursuers.

Not that it would take the four of them long to figure out that I was no longer following the river that cut through the narrow valley. These guys were hunters who specialized in tracking down a particular category of prey—the two-legged kind—and, right now, I was their prey.

My only hope was to get to the top of the hill sot that I might be able to see some landmark that would tell me where the hell I was, and help me plot out the best route to safety. Maybe, if I was lucky, I'd also get a cell phone signal.

Of course, with a shot up leg, and weak from the loss of blood before I'd been able to stop it with my mud-leaf poultice, there was a good chance they'd discover my route and catch up to me before I ever reached the top of the next hill. Hell, there was a good chance that I was so weak from loss of blood I'd pass out before I got to the bottom of the little valley between me and the base of the hill. If that happened, I was a goner.

I shook my head to clear it of such negative thoughts, which wasn't a good idea in my current condition. I almost toppled over. If I hadn't been leaning back against the tree trunk, I would have.

Okay, no more sudden movements. But, also, no more negative thoughts. I could get out of this. I'd been in tight spots before. Well, I *hadn't* been shot before, but I had been in life-threatening situations, with the odds no in my favor, and I'd survived. Damnit, I could do it again. No. I *would* do it again.

I just needed to find a safe place to hole up until the pain in my leg subsided and my strength came back. It would have helped if I'd known where I was, which is always a good idea when someone's chasing you and you're trying to get to safety.

I mean, I knew in a general way where I was. In Garrett County, Maryland's westernmost and least populated county, a mostly rural place that identified more with West Virginia than Maryland, and whose closest big city was Pittsburgh, Pennsylvania. I was somewhere south of the Mason-Dixon Line, which, for the record, has nothing to do with dividing the north from the south as many people think, but was surveyed by Charles Mason and Jeremiah Dixon between 1763 and 1767 to resolve land claims among Maryland, Pennsylvania, and Delaware when they were still English colonies. I'd been running along the Youghiogheny River, north of the little town of Oakland, but with the relatively open banks, I was too easy a target, and a lucky shot from one of my pursuers had entered the fleshy outside part of my left thigh and exited through the front. Luckily, it hadn't hit bone or blood vessel, but it had bled like hell nonetheless, and like I said, hurt like bloody hell. I heard the 'pop' of a handgun almost at the same time I felt the white hot sensation as the slug passed through my leg. If he'd had an assault rifle, or a larger caliber handgun, it would probably have taken me down. He'd been lucky to even hit me from over three hundred feet away. It's hard to hit a moving target with a handgun up close, and damn near impossible at that distance. Near impossible, though, is not the same as totally impossible, and I had two holes in my leg to prove it.

My pursuers had been on the far side of the river, and by the time they'd backtracked to the suspension bridge I'd used to cross it, I'd patched up my wound and moved farther uphill, but not before gathering up an armful of bloody leaves and leaving a trail going up river. My hope was they'd assume I'd stay on the easier lower ground with my wound, or maybe even pass out and fall into the river and drown.

Of course, they wouldn't stop looking until they found a body. They couldn't afford to let me get away. If I got away, it would throw a huge monkey wrench in their plans. Now, that I could get behind, except, what I wanted to do is take a monkey wrench to certain sensitive parts of their anatomy.

Does that sound like I'd decided that maybe I wouldn't die after all? Bet your sweet ass it does.

I would not only survive, but I would make these bastards pay, and not just for what they'd done to me. Although, shooting me was, in my mind, justification enough. Shooting an unarmed man is not a very nice thing to do. When that unarmed man is me, it's an even bigger mistake not to kill him with the first shot.

I could feel myself getting angry, so angry in fact that the pain in my thigh was now just a dull ache. With the anger, my vision began to clear. It was time to get moving.

It would have been nice to have a map of the terrain. When I was in the army, I never went on an operation without first doing a map recon of the operational area. Of course, when I took this job just over a week ago, it never occurred to me that I would need a map.

Chapter
Two

March 6, 2003, just off River Road, near Potomac, Maryland

I'd just kissed Sandra goodbye and was heading out the door when the phone rang.

If I'd had a landline and an answering machine, I would have ignored it, or if it had been Sandra's phone. But, it was my cell phone that was ringing. In addition to the warbling ringing sound, I could feel it vibrating against my side through my jacket pocket.

"Are you going to answer that?" Sandra asked. The tone in her voice said that *not* answering was probably not a good idea.

And, she was probably right. She'd been right in thinking I didn't want to answer. I hate talking on the phone. Disembodied little voices in my ear drive me nuts because I can't see the faces and body language of the speaker to help me sort the truth from the mostly bullshit that people spew at you on a daily basis.

Sandra walked over to me, a determined *why aren't you answering my question* look on her face. On some people that look would be unattractive. On her it made me want to rip her clothes off and take her right there in the living room.

But, if I did that, she'd be late for school. If that happened, things on the home front would get frosty. I could see her giving that look to her students, and could imagine their reaction. "Yes, Miss Winter," they would say. "Of course I'm going to answer it." She could melt a glacier with that look.

Besides, I don't give my number to that many people, so chances were it was business related. And, business is what I'm about.

While Sandra teaches language arts at Carver High School, an inner city school in one of Washington, DC's poorest neighborhoods, I, Al Pennyback, am a private investigator. My partner, Heather Bunche, and I are 'A. E. Pennyback, Confidential Enquiries,' and we work the mean streets, highways, and backroads of the Washington Metropolitan Area, which consists of the District, Northern Virginia, and suburban Maryland. We get a nice hundred grand a month retainer from a law firm to do scut work for them, and the occasional over the transom client with an interesting case. Our over the transom cases aren't usually from among the hand full of people who have my number, and I don't do a lot of social calling.

"Yeah, I guess I should," I said, pulling the phone from my pocket.

She gave me a look I'm sure she gave dozens of times each day to the students at Carver, and turned away to get her purse.

"Hello," I said into the phone.

"Al, Quincy here, I have a job for you."

There was no need for him to say that. As soon as I recognized his voice, I knew it was business. Quincy Chang is a senior partner with Holcombe, Stein and Chang, the law firm that has me on a ten thousand buck per month retainer, and an old army buddy. He's also one of my closest friends, and like me, he's not given to social phone calls.

"Must be important for you to call me at home," I said.

He made a throat clearing sound. "It's time sensitive. I need you to meet me somewhere before you go to your office."

I didn't pick up any tension in his voice, but it had to be important to get Quincy going at 7:00 a.m.

"Can you tell me what this is about?"

"I'd rather not go into it on the phone. I'll explain everything when I see you."

That got my attention, and my look of confusion got Sandra's attention.

She mouthed at me 'what's up?', and I shrugged and shook my head.

"Okay," I said. "Give me the address."

Chapter
Three

The address Quincy gave me was on Kendale Road, off Bradley Boulevard, which is one of the main streets that intersect River Road between my place and the I-495 Beltway. Sandra and I left home at the same time, and I followed her up River Road until I had to make the left turn onto Bradley. I flashed my lights at her, and she waved. I noticed a fat, bald man with a newspaper draped over his steering wheel, who was sitting in a silver BMW on Bradley waiting for the light to turn onto River Road, give me a strange look as I drove past him. I guess the sight of a six-foot-plus dark brown skinned man waving at a statuesque blue-eyed blonde struck him as unusual. It shouldn't have. We have a lot of Indian and other South Asian millionaires living in the Potomac area, some of whom are many shades darker than me. Of course, none of them have wives or girlfriends (if they have girlfriends) who are not also South Asian. Oh well, not my problem.

I drove half a mile northeast on Bradley and turned left onto Kendale. It was a winding, tree-lined, two-lane street that was perpetually shaded by the canopy of limbs and leaves where the trees on each side met overhead. Many of the houses were behind high brick or stone walls and not visible from the street. Those that were spoke of money—loudly, and with many zeroes. In suburbia, a two-car garage is a status symbol. On this street, the smallest garage I saw had four doors.

The address Quincy had given me was one of the ones behind a high stone wall. Black metal double gates were firmly anchored to the wall. An intercom on a metal pole sat on the left side of the pebbled driveway. I stopped, lowered my window and waited. After thirty seconds nothing had happened. Then, I noticed the black button beneath the speaker grille. I pressed the button.

It didn't make a sound for several seconds. Then, a tinny voice said, "Please state your name and business."

"Al Pennyback," I said. "I'm supposed to meet Quincy Chang here."

"Yes, you're expected. Please wait for the gate to open completely, and then drive through. Follow the drive and park on the concrete pad you'll see to your right."

There was a pop and sizzle of static and then a whirring sound as the black metal gates started swinging inward. I started driving forward as soon as the gap was wide enough for my Volkswagen bug to slip through. If anyone was watching and were upset, I'd deal with that later. I'm six feet tall and weigh two-ten, so unless there was a platoon of security goons armed with AK-47s waiting for me, I figured I could handle it.

The gates started swinging close almost as soon as the rear end of my car cleared them. So much for waiting until the gates were fully open.

The driveway was wide enough for two cars, and lined on both sides by a knee-high hedge. Beyond the hedge on both sides, the lawn stretched away, a long way away, and was dotted with topiary shaped like angels, animals, and some shapes that looked like they'd been inspired by J.R.R. Tolkien. The driveway curved slightly to the left and sloped slightly uphill and as I made the turn the house came into view.

It was humongous. Three stories high and almost a city block wide. Pink stone with a blood red roof and off-white window shutters, it had a large entrance with a stone canopy over the drive that circled around, past the entrance and looped back onto itself. The second and third floor had balconies with marble rails. Well-tended flower beds clung to the base of the building. Off to the right, just as the disembodied voice had said, was a large paved area the size of two tennis courts, and I saw Quincy's black Lexus ES 300. His was the only car. Just beyond the parking pad, adjacent to the house and connected with the driveway by a paved drive was a building with six large doors, which I assumed to be a garage. I wondered if there was a car behind every door, and figured there probably was. At the far end of the lawn on the left was a small cottage; small only in comparison to the main house. The one-story Cape Cod house was as big as my farm house. My guess: servants' quarters.

Whoever lived here was loaded. But then, if he was a client of Quincy's firm, that was a given.

I parked next to Quincy's car and hoofed it to the front of the house.

The door was the same color as the roof. There was a doorbell button to the side, but also a door knocker, a big brass lion's head with a ring in its mouth. I pushed the doorbell button. The muffled opening notes of Beethoven's 'fur Elise' came through the door. I love the song, but have never understood why people think it makes an appropriate door chime.

I heard clicking sounds, followed by a 'snick,'

and then the door swung inward.

A thin man wearing a black waistcoat and a bored expression stood there with one hand on the door and the other on his hip. Even though he was only about five-six or seven, he looked down his aquiline nose at me.

"Mr. Pennyback," he said in a posh New England accent. "Mr. Chang and the master are waiting for you in the salon. Please come this way."

He stepped aside for me to enter, and when I did he closed the door, spun on his tiny heels and proceeded toward the back of the house. I followed him. The entrance foyer, eight feet wide and about twelve feet deep, was a simple affair. On the left wall was a large mirror, next to which was a closed door to what I assumed was a closet. On the right was a small table upon which was a round silver tray. It took me a moment to take that in, and then I realized that this was a tray for calling cards. Whoever Quincy's client was, he was a definite throwback to a bygone age. Farther on in the foyer, open doors to the right and left, led to a sun room and a small sitting room respectively. The foyer floor was polished off-white marble with black veins running through it. Our shoes made clicking sounds as we walked, sounds that echoed off the dark, unadorned walls. It felt like walking into a mausoleum. The only thing needed to complete the impression would have been the sound of a funeral dirge coming from hidden speakers.

Charles Ray

At the end of the foyer, we stepped into a giant open room with chairs and small tables around the walls, and a crystal chandelier the size of my Volkswagen suspended from the center of the vaulted ceiling. The walls were off-white and had gooseneck lights above expensive looking paintings and prints all around. I've been in museums with fewer paintings.

My guide hung a right, and I eye-balled the paintings on the wall as we passed them. I'm no art expert, but they looked like originals. Some of the frames were scratched and pitted with age, and one of the etchings was a bit wrinkled as if it had suffered water damage. I didn't recognize any of them, but like I said, they didn't look like reproductions.

At the end of that side of the room, we came to a door. My guide opened it and stepped aside, bowing. I took that to mean I was to enter, so I did.

Chapter
Four

The room I entered was about twice the size of the entrance foyer. On the left was a large, kidney-shaped desk made of dark mahogany. Behind it was a brown leather executive chair with cushioned arms. On the surface were a leather and felt desk pad and a pen and pencil set that glinted gold under the light from an old fashioned lamp that sat on the corner, casting light on the desk pad. Behind the desk was a waist-high credenza with several stacks of manila folders neatly arranged on its top.

Directly in front of me was a floor-to-ceiling bookcase filled with leather bound books. On the right I saw a coffee table, similar in shape and construction to the desk, flanked by two overstuffed chairs and with a two-cushion sofa against the wall.

Quincy, with a cup halfway to his mouth, sat in the chair facing the door. He looked up as I entered, and when I saw the man sitting on the sofa, he smiled at the look of shock that flickered briefly on my face.

I caught myself and composed my expression, making it as neutral as I could manage, which wasn't easy.

To say the man sitting on the sofa was fat would be like saying the Grand Canyon is deep. He took up the whole sofa, and parts of his gigantic butt hung over each side. He wore a purple dressing gown that could have easily doubled as a cover for a king-sized bed, and the foot that I could see, his left foot, barely fit into a slipper that both of my size elevens could have slipped into. His head was as round as a basketball, and not much smaller, with jowls that brushed the collar of his dressing gown, and his eyes were nearly invisible in the puffy flesh of his cheeks and brows. His thin brown hair was brushed straight back, and I could see the pink flesh of his skull. In my mind I was thinking that this is what Humpty Dumpty would look like if he was a man. The cup he held was barely visible in a hand bigger than two of mine, and I'm not a small person.

Quincy composed himself as well. Putting on his lawyer face, he looked at me over the rim of his cup.

"Glad you could make it, Al," he said. "Mr. Boulware, this is Al Pennyback, the private investigator I told you about. Al, this is my client, Chester Boulware."

Boulware nodded and blew over his cup through fleshy pink lips. He didn't offer to shake hands.

"Welcome, Mr. Pennyback," he said. His voice was deep and resonant. "Please, sit down. Would you like some tea? We're having chamomile."

I'm not a tea drinker, despite Heather's best efforts to wean me off coffee, but it would have been rude to refuse.

"Sure, tea would be fine."

He put his cup down and reached for a delicate china tea pot sitting in the middle of the table. With more dexterity than I would've thought a man of his bulk capable he filled an empty cup and pushed it across the table toward me as I sat in the empty chair.

"Would you like sugar or milk?"

"No, thanks," I said. "I'll take it black."

I lifted the cup, blew on it, and took a sip. It wasn't bad, but I would have preferred coffee.

"I suppose you're wondering what this is all about," Quincy said.

"Yeah, the thought did cross my mind."

He looked at Boulware. "Perhaps you'd like to explain, Chester?"

Boulware pouted and put his cup down on the table. "Always business first, Quincy, and I assume your friend here is the same," he said. "I get company so seldom, it's nice to just sit, chat, and enjoy a nice cup of tea." At Quincy's frown, he held up his meaty hands in surrender. "Oh, very well, if we must."

He took his time adjusting the lapels of his dressing gown. Then, he turned his tiny eyes toward me.

"As you no doubt surmised as you were walking here from the entrance," he said. "I am an art collector. I have perhaps the most extensive collection of art in this area, if not the entire country."

I hadn't surmised any such thing, but I sensed that it was important to him, so I nodded. He didn't seem to notice or care.

"There is, however, one painting that has forever eluded me, a painting by Van Gogh. If I had that my collection would be complete."

I gave Quincy a hard look. He looked as confused as I was feeling, and shrugged.

"I'm a private investigator, Mr. Boulware, not an art dealer. I don't see how I can be of any help to you."

Now it was Boulware's turn to glare at Quincy. "I thought you said he was tough and reliable?"

"He is," Quincy said. "But, you have to be a bit clearer on what it is you want him to do."

"Do you know?" I asked Quincy.

He shook his head. "No, he just said he

needed someone reliable and able to deal with rugged situations." He glared back at Boulware. "Now, maybe it would be a good idea of you told *both* of us just what it is you want Al to do."

"I suppose you're correct. I can't have Mr. Pennyback running around completely blind, now can I?" He reached into his pocket and pulled out a piece of paper. He held it up, looking at it. "As I said, Mr. Pennyback, I have an extensive art collection. It needs just one more piece to be complete. I've been searching for that piece for three decades, and I finally have a lead on it. I want you to retrieve it for me."

"I told you, I'm not an art dealer. Surely there's someone else you could send to fetch your precious painting."

He shook his head, setting his jowls to quivering.

"If only it were that simple," he said. "This painting is priceless, and it will cost me a great deal of money. I need someone I can trust to deliver that money and get that painting back safely to me. I've dealt with a lot of art dealers, but there are none that I would trust with this amount of money."

"What amount?" I asked.

"Three quarters of a million dollars," he said.

I swallowed hard.

"You're right, that's a lot of money."

"Quincy assures me that you're a man of integrity, and while losing that much money wouldn't put me in the poor house, you can understand that I would prefer not to turn it over to just anyone."

"I guess that makes sense, but it's not the kind of case I usually take."

"Would you take it for one hundred thousand dollars?"

They say that everyone has a price. He'd found mine. He wasn't asking me to kill anyone or rob a bank, just be a messenger boy. Well, for a hundred grand I'd swallow my pride and be a delivery boy.

Chapter
Five

After I agreed to take the job, Boulware relaxed and resumed drinking his tea. He handed me the paper, which was an old black and white photo of a painting of some old guy walking down a country road. The person or persons with the painting hadn't given him a drop location, so we decided that we'd wait for that before he gave me the money. That was fine by me. Running around with that much money wasn't something I relished.

I carefully folded the paper and put it in my jacket with my phone, then took a deep breath and shook Boulware's hand.

Outside, Quincy tried to apologize, but I assured him there was no problem. We drove in convoy back into the District, with him peeling off of Whitehurst Freeway toward K Street and me heading across town to my office on Fourth Street just south of the Waterfront Metro Station.

The offices of A.E. Pennyback, Confidential Enquiries is on the second floor of an old brick and wood frame building that looks a lot like a roadside motel. The small businesses that inhabit the building come and go on a regular basis. Currently, we were sandwiched between a CPA and an architect. I'd never met either of my neighbors, and since they probably wouldn't be around long, didn't bother to introduce myself. I parked in one of the three spaces in front of the building that were reserved for us. With Heather's car in another, that only left one for any customer who drove, but in all the years we'd been in business I don't think anyone had ever used it. I hadn't locked my car when I parked at Boulware's, but I made sure to lock it in front of my office.

The neighborhood's being gentrified, with condos and office towers going up all over the place, but it still has a rough element. An unlocked car is an invitation to have it stolen.

Upstairs, Heather was waiting for me with a frown on her pixie-like face.

"Banker's hours today? You could have at least called and let me know you'd be late."

Oops. "Sorry, partner," I said. "But I was out getting us a case, and it just slipped my mind."

"I believe they call that having a senior moment," she said. That was the first time she'd played the age card since I turned fifty three years earlier.

"Yeah, maybe, but how does a fee of a hundred grand sound?"

Her mouth made a not so little 'O'.

"What do you have to do for that much?"

I told her, and her eyes went as round as her mouth.

"That's it?" she asked. "That's all you have to do. Go somewhere, give someone some money, and deliver a painting to this guy?"

"That's it."

She shook her head. "There has to be a catch. No one, not even a millionaire pays that much just for a delivery job."

I hadn't thought about that. Hell, after Boulware dropped the sum one hundred thousand, I must have stopped thinking. Heather was right. Something didn't add up. We humans, though, are strange. When we've made our minds up, we look for any excuse to justify the decision, no matter how ill-advised.

"This guy struck me as a bit on the eccentric side," I said. "He's so fat, I don't think he gets out of his house much but he has a six-car garage."

The look she gave me told me how stupid *that*

sounded, but I wasn't ready to give up.

"He's just an eccentric old guy with money to burn?"

She still didn't look convinced.

"Are you saying I shouldn't have taken the case?"

"No, I'm not saying that." She flipped a lock of blonde hair from in front of her eyes. Lately, she'd taken to wearing her hair long like Sandra. "I mean, a hundred thousand, that's a lot of money. I'm just saying that something doesn't smell right about this."

Hindsight, they say, is twenty-twenty. Now that her words were finally penetrating the barrier that's my thick skull, I realized she was right. Rich or eccentric, people don't just throw that much money out willy-nilly. There was something behind the curtain.

Now, having come to that brilliant conclusion, you'd probably think I'd call Quincy or the client and back out of the case. You'd be wrong. First, I'd given my word, and I don't go back on my word lightly. Second, thanks to Heather's concerns, this had become a puzzling situation, and I'm a total sucker for puzzles.

"You're right," I said. "So, while we wait for the pickup address, why don't you do your magic and find out all you can about our client."

"What am I looking for?"

"Doh! What I just said—everything, and I mean everything. Do the full background on this guy, and see if there's anything in his background that's shady."

"And, while I'm doing that, what will you be doing?"

I like to think I'm the brains of our operation, but the fact is, I'm just the muscle. Heather, with her ability to coax obscure information from that mysterious realm she calls cyberspace, or to get people to confide their most intimate details to her—over the phone no less, is really the brains. Until Boulware gave me more information there wasn't a thing for me to do but sit around twiddling my thumbs.

"I suppose I could call Buster and ask him to have lunch with me at Mom's."

Buster is Buster Mayweather, a detective with the DC Metro police, and a friend since coming to my house and informing me of the death of my wife and son in a senseless traffic accident, and Mom's is a soul food restaurant near the U Street/Sixteenth Street intersection that we frequently visit when our cholesterol counts get too low. Whenever I mention Mom's Heather grimaces.

"Bored out of your skull with nothing to do, right?"

"Buster might know something about our client."

She looked at her watch.

"It's too early for lunch."

It was 10:30, and even driving slow, it wouldn't take me more than thirty minutes to get to Mom's.

"So, we'll just do brunch," I said.

Charles Ray

Chapter
Six

As I'd anticipated, Buster immediately accepted my invitation to an early lunch, and forty-five minutes later we were sitting at our usual table at Mom's, the one in the front corner where we could both have our backs to a wall, watch the street outside through the big plate glass window, and keep an eye on the inside at the same time. Neither of us liked to sit where we could be blindsided, me from years in the army doing special operations missions in some pretty nasty places, and him from years on the streets as a DC cop.

Mom, all three hundred pounds of her, hovered over us, temporarily blocking our view.

"Y'all want coffee or ice tea with your meal?" she asked in her still pronounced southern accent and younger than she looked voice.

She never asked us what we wanted *for* our meal, only what we wanted to drink *with* it. At Mom's you ate what she told you to eat.

"I'll have iced tea, no sugar, and a twist of lemon," I said. She gave me the evil eye. Where Mom comes from—somewhere way south of Richmond, Virginia, no one drinks tea without enough sugar in it to make it glisten in the sunlight.

"I'll have tea, too," Buster said. "But, put three spoons of sugar in mine." She gave him a motherly smile and patted his head.

He couldn't resist gloating at me. Usually Mom treats me like the 'good' son, and he gets the sharp edge of her tongue. He was stilling smiling like the Cheshire cat when she returned with our drinks.

"Y'all just go on and enjoy this while your food's cookin'," she said, and patted his shoulder while looking at me and frowning.

When she'd gone he picked his glass up and took a long drink, then put it down and wiped his lips with the back of his hand.

"Man, that sure is sweet," he said.

"The tea or Mom preferring you over me?"

"Both. Now, you want to tell me why we meetin' for lunch on Thursday instead of hump day or Friday like we usually do?"

Buster sometimes acts like he's slow, but just like the ghetto speech pattern he puts on, it's all an act. He has a mind every bit as sharp as mine. I told him about Chester Boulware and the job he wanted me to do.

"What's this dude up to?" he asked when I'd finished.

"Meaning?"

"I know you say the dude's rich, but that's a lotta bread for a simple delivery. What's he got cookin'?"

"He told Quincy it was because he wanted someone he could trust with that much money. He's one of Quincy's clients."

Buster rubbed at his square jaw.

"Hell, there's no shortage of bonded delivery companies in DC he could've hired for a lot less than a hundred grand. I don't know, Al. Something sounds fishy about this whole deal."

"Yeah, Heather said pretty much the same. I have her checking the guy's background. Have you ever heard of him?"

"Hey, a guy like that ain't likely to ever been on my radar. Now, if he was a gang banger or street punk . . ."

"I was just wondering . . . maybe you could check with some of your sources?"

He sat back in his chair and folded his muscular arms across his massive chest.

"Uh, I don't know, bro. We start checking on this guy and he's done nothing . . . well, you know how that could go."

I did know how it could go. Whether Boulware was clean or dirty—and, especially if he was dirty—if word somehow got to him that a lowly DC cop was checking up on him, said cop could find himself directing traffic in Anacostia. But, I also knew that Buster, like Heather, had ways of discretely getting information, and for reasons I couldn't have explained, I felt it was important for him to do so.

"You said you thought something was hinky about this deal," I reminded him. "Couldn't you just do a little light checking?"

"Yeah, I did say something smelled, didn't I?" He rubbed his chin again. "Well, I guess I could ask around a little. If I hear anything, I'll give you a call."

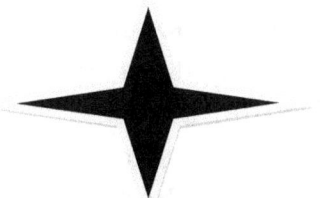

Chapter
Seven

"It's like he doesn't exist," Heather said. Exasperation contorted her otherwise beautiful face. "I can't find even one mention of him on any of the sites I've searched."

That didn't sound good, not good at all. No one, and I mean *no* one, with as much money as Boulware had—or at least what his house and the way he talked about money indicated could be unknown. I'd come to believe that everyone was somewhere in that vast region called cyberspace. Credit card purchases, property deeds, and for someone like Boulware and his art collection, the occasional news article; it was all supposed to be there in some electronic file. But, Heather's not one to exaggerate. If she said she couldn't find anything that meant it wasn't there.

"Maybe you're not looking in the right places," I said, knowing as soon as I did that it was grasping at straws, and was an insult to her computer skills.

She gave me a look that said she *was* insulted. "I've looked at *every possible* site, social media, news sites, even a few of those name look-up sites. He's not there. I can't find a phone number, social security number, address . . . nothing."

"Did you check drivers' licenses or car registrations?"

"Of course. Nothing there."

"I was at the guy's house," I said. "He lives in a mansion and has a six-car garage and at least one servant. What about utilities?" I gave her the address. "See who pays the light bills."

Her eyes lit up and the dour expression vanished in an instant. "Darn it, why didn't I think of that? I've been looking for *him* by name. I forgot to do a reverse address look-up."

I restrained a smile. It's not often I get one up on her in the computer department. Of course, it had nothing to do with my computer skills, which are nil, but it's what I would've done in the old days when the only way to get information was to dig through dusty paper files."

"Okay," she said. "Go into your office and leave me alone. I'll let you know what I find."

Dismissed, I went into my office and plopped down in the scuffed leather executive chair behind my scuffed mahogany executive desk, both of which I'd picked up at a military surplus auction when I opened the office. Along with the autographed picture of former Chairman of the Joint Chiefs of Staff General Colin Powell that had been given to me when I served as a colonel at the Pentagon, they were the only original items still there. Over the years Heather had piece by piece replaced everything else.

One of the new things she'd foisted off on me was a thin Hewlett-Packard laptop computer. Damn thing was about the side of a thick college composition book and, according to Heather, had the computing power of a room full of the old computers I'd seen, but never used, when I was in the army, just as the Defense Department was switching from IBM Selectric typewriters to desktop computers. When I'm idle, which was what I was at the moment, I usually turn it on and play chess. The machine always beats me, but I keep trying.

But, I really didn't feel like playing chess. So, I did my next favorite thing; I swiveled my chair around and looked out the window. In early March, and after a fairly cold winter, the trees between the towering condos hadn't sprouted a full crown of leaves yet, so I had a good view of the little slice of the Washington Channel and the Potomac River between the tall buildings. I could see the masts of sailboats in the channel and the occasional plane coming in for a landing at National Airport, now renamed Reagan National Airport after the B-movie actor turned president.

The sight of a few masts gliding along, the hardy sailors willing to brave the chilly March breezes blowing up the Potomac, and more than happy to have the river to themselves, because by June, when the oppressive Washington area heat settles in, the river's like a sauna, helped to calm my chaotic thoughts. Chaotic, that is, for me. I was running a number of scenarios through my mind, none of them particularly pleasing. Boulware was one of Quincy's clients, which should have been validation enough, but why would information on him be so scarce. Most of the firm's clients were all over the news, print and electronic, giving to charities, showing up at fancy parties, or buying and selling companies. This guy was a Black Swan; that outlying event or entity that didn't fit any normal criteria. He was an enigma, which is a fancy word for puzzle. While I was earning the generous fee he'd offered for a routine task, I was determined to solve the puzzle—free of charge. That's just how I am.

Then, I realized that there *was* something I could do. I pulled out my cell phone and hit the speed dial button for Quincy's number.

"Holcombe, Stein and Chang, Mr. Chang's office, how may I help you?" Quincy's personal assistant, an elderly woman with on overactive libido—she propositioned me every time I visited his office—and a penchant for frequently changing her hair color, answered with a tone that reminded me of a librarian, stern and forbidding.

"Al Pennyback for Mr. Chang," I said.

"Oh, the delightful Mr. Pennyback. How can *I* be of service to *you*?" Now she sounded like the female lead from an old 1940s film noir.

Usually, I played along with her, but today I had a mission and no time for her games. At the same time, I wasn't about to alienate her. Personal assistants are the ultimate gatekeepers. Piss them off and you find yourself locked out. "You could put me through to Quincy," I said. "And, I'll think of something for the next time I drop by."

"I'll hold you to that," she said. "And, I do mean *hold* you. Hang on, I'll connect you."

I heard a soft laugh just before the ubiquitous 'hold' music came on. She played the game well. I think I was the highlight of her day.

A few seconds later, Quincy came on the

line. "What's up, Al?"

"Quince, I have a slight problem with your . . . our client."

"Have you heard from him about the pick-up?"

"No, but that's not the problem."

There was a long pause, and then he cleared his throat. "You mean the fact that you can't find him in any of the usual data bases Heather searches." It was a statement not a question. He knew that there were no records on Boulware.

"You knew this? You knew it, and you didn't bother to tell me?"

Again, a pause. "I, uh, knew you, or Heather, would discover that little situation. I debated telling you, but I wasn't sure how you'd take it. From the tone of your voice, I gather you're not taking it well. Does this mean you're changing your mind about the job?"

Now, I made him wait a few seconds. I wasn't mad at him, just a little disappointed, and I wanted to make him squirm a bit. Finally, I said, "No, I haven't changed my mind about the job, but I want you to tell me everything you know about Boulware. Oh, and when this is all over, I'm gonna get you for holding out on me."

"And, I won't like what you do, right?"

"That's the point, amigo, now spill."

"Okay, but I can't tell you much more than you already know," he said, and then proceeded to tell me a lot more than I already knew, I just didn't realize it at the time. "Chester Boulware's been a client of this firm for the past five years. He contacted us by phone and asked specifically for me, and insisted I meet him at his house."

The reason for that odd request, Quincy found, was that Boulware was morbidly obese; but, the main thing was that he was a recluse who informed Quincy that he *never* left his house except for the occasional walk around inside the walled estate. Boulware had informed him that he was sixty, making him sixty-five presently. It was hard to tell with someone his size, but he hadn't looked that old to me. Boulware had no social security number, and wouldn't tell Quincy where he'd been born or where he'd gone to school, claiming that this was not information Quincy needed in order to represent his legal interests. Quincy had balked at first, but like me, had found his price. Boulware paid Holcombe, Stein and Chang a retainer of five hundred grand a month—or rather, a blind trust paid it—and Quincy had only had to do anything on perhaps ten occasions over the five years they'd represented the man. When I asked what kind of legal work had been done, Quincy said mostly certifying documents of authenticity for works of art. On one occasion he'd been asked to certify a document in which one Chester Boulware attested that he was, in fact, Chester Boulware.

"Isn't this a bit unusual, even for eccentric rich people?" I asked when he'd finished.

"A decade ago, or when you and I were in the army, I would have said yes," he replied. "But, since then, I've done enough wills with poodles as heirs not to question what some of our clients do. As long as they stay within the law, I no longer ask questions, I just collect the fees and move on."

I wasn't quite ready to let it go, though. "Surely, though, a client who insists on staying completely off the radar must have triggered some kind of warning."

"Like I said, we have a lot of clients who are off the weird scale. In Chester's case, we did a criminal records check, and he came back clean. One look at him explained his reluctance to be in public. In other words, other than no driver's license, no credit cards, and no social security number, there was nothing strange."

"I guess I can see the driver's license and credit card, but how the hell does he get away with not having a social security number? I thought they were required for everyone who pays taxes."

"They are, but he doesn't, and never has, so it's never been an issue. He's also never been claimed as a dependent on a tax return. Apparently, he's got some kind of trust that pays corporate taxes. It covers his living expenses, including his art collection, and since he's not employed—according to him, he's *never* been gainfully employed—he's never had to file any kind of tax return."

"Wow!" That was all I could say. I wouldn't have thought it possible that someone could achieve it. Totally absent from the world of records and files, as if he'd never existed. I was working for the invisible man. Considering Boulware's bulk, that was funny, but I didn't think Quincy would appreciate the humor. "Okay," I said. "I'm still a little miffed at you for not sharing this information up front, but I'll do the job."

"Thanks, Al. Look, if it's any consolation, Chester sprang this on me that morning while I was having my first cup of coffee. It didn't seem like a subject to talk to you about over the phone, and you can understand why I didn't bring it up at his house."

"Yeah, but you could've told me about it afterwards."

"Uh, mea culpa. It just slipped my mind. I've been working with him so long, I seldom even think about it anymore."

I still wasn't letting him off the hook. I would have to think of an appropriate punishment. For now, though, I'd just let him sweat. "Okay, Quince," I said. "Talk to you later."

I broke the connection and stuffed the phone back into my shirt pocket. Just as I was turning my chair back toward the window, Heather walked in.

"I looked up the information you suggested," she said. Her brow was wrinkled and she was frowning. "And, it just keeps getting stranger and stranger."

Chapter
Eight

"The deed to the property is in the name of a holding company, Essex Enterprises, which is also the entity that pays the taxes, utilities, and any other costs associated with it. The same company holds the titles to six luxury cars, and the driver of record for those cars is one Jarvis McKenna, who I assume is the chauffeur. He uses a credit card to pay for gas and repairs, and it goes on for everything else associated with the house and grounds," Heather said. "Chester Boulware's name does not appear on any document or file associated with that place."

I told her what I'd learned from Quincy. She shook her head and shot me a look of disbelief.

"No one can be alive and be completely off the grid," she said. "There has to be a birth certificate somewhere, at the very least."

She was right about that. Even if he'd been born outside the United States; if he was a foreigner, there'd be an immigration record of his entry, and if he was born abroad to American citizen parents, there'd be the record of his birth completed by the local American consular officer and subsequent entry into the United States. I mentioned that to her.

"Immigration records aren't easy to access without a court order," she said. "But, I'll look into that. That, though, wasn't what's really odd about his finances."

"Oh, what could be odder than a man who doesn't seem to officially exist?"

"When I tried tracking down names associated with Essex Enterprises, which by the way is registered in Delaware, a haven for fly-by-night companies, I found that it's owned by yet another holding company, Phoenix Corporation, which is registered in the Cayman Islands."

"Who owns Phoenix Corporation?"

"Good question. I can't find any mention of them anywhere other than the files on Essex."

"Surely there are banking records or something."

"Yes, but the only banking records I can access just mention Essex. Phoenix Corporation is like a ghost, a lot like Boulware himself."

"What about records in the Caymans, can you access them?"

"I can, but it won't be easy." She looked worried. "It's not as easy to get into computer files outside the country as you think, that, and the fact that the banking laws in the Caymans makes it a prime place for people to put their money when they don't want anyone else to know about it, means their computer systems are harder to get into than the Pentagon."

That made sense. When you're banker for gangsters and dictators, you'd better be able to protect their assets if you valued your ass. I didn't envy a customer relations officer for a bank in the Caymans.

"You're gonna keep trying, though, right?"

"Well, of course I am," she said. "No one can be completely invisible. Mr. Boulware and this Phoenix Corporation have left a bread crumb somewhere out there, and I'm going to find it."

Charles Ray

Chapter
Nine

Heather's like a bloodhound—or maybe a pit bull. Once she gets a scent, she never lets up. In her own way, she's as maniacal as me about puzzles. While she did her magic with the computer, though, I had another avenue to follow. Chester Boulware and Phoenix Corporation were hiding something, or something was hiding them, and whenever I encountered this kind of mystery, my go-to resource was the one person I know who is familiar with 'black' operations. Carlton

Raine, nicknamed 'Blood' by his former colleagues, was a retired CIA operative, one of the first black men to be hired by the agency as a full-fledged field agent, back in the day when the ranks of the intelligence agencies were pretty much vanilla. He'd served in some of the hottest spots on the planet, and with distinction. He got his nickname because during many of his operations copious quantities of blood flowed.

Now in his eighties, he still retained contact with some people in the agency, people whose names he'd never disclosed, and they often 'loaned' him equipment they were field testing, for his evaluation.

I first encountered Raine when I was dodging a Chinese gangster I'd help put in prison. The man was out and looking for revenge by targeting people close to me. Thanks to some of Raine's toys, Buster and I brought the gangster down—permanently.

As a result of that case, I'd introduced Raine to Elizabeth Sung, a Chinese-American lawyer who'd gotten caught up in the whole mess and needed a safe place to stay—and, believe me, no place in the area is safer than Raine's cabin in the woods, except maybe the White House. Anyway, they took a liking to each other, and have been a couple since, and Raine and I have been friends since. I like to think it's because he sees a little of his younger self in me, but I'm enough of a realist to know that a large part of it is his way of thanking me for bringing Elizabeth into his life.

I left the office early, drove past the turnoff to my place, and kept going west on River Road until I came to the unmarked turnoff on the right that's the road to Raine's *pied a tierre.*

As I usually do when I drive along the sandy road to Raine's cabin I tried spotting the surveillance camera I know he has hidden in the trees alongside, and as usual, I couldn't see a thing. And, as usual, he was standing on his front porch waiting for me when I rounded the last turn in the road and saw his cabin, a log structure sitting in a clearing with nothing over two feet high for over a hundred yards in all directions.

"Hey, young fellow, what brings you my way?" He didn't say, without calling first, which I usually do.

I got out of the car and walked to the porch, where I grasped his angular, but still strong, hand in a warm grip.

"Sorry for not calling in advance," I said. "But, I was distracted by my current case. I'm not interrupting anything, am I?"

"No, Liz is in San Francisco for some kind of legal conference, so I'm here all by myself. I appreciate the company. I have a pot of coffee on . . . Jamaican, the kind you like, with a hint of chicory . . . come on in and join me."

I *love* coffee, especially Jamaican or Colombian, and Raine makes it even better than I do.

"I could use a cup," I said, following him inside the cabin.

The inside is a lot more spacious than you'd think looking at the place from the outside. The big living room, with a large sofa facing the door and a low coffee table in front of that, placed such that anyone rushing through the door will have to slow and turn to keep from banging into the table, stretched across the width of the building. In the center of the wall behind the sofa is a heavy metal door which leads to his command center which contains the screens through which he can monitor the entire property, and his armory. A door to the right leads to the bedroom and bath and one to the left to the kitchen and small dining nook. A credenza to the right of the sofa had a silver coffee urn and two large white ceramic mugs. He'd probably added the second mug when his early warning system alerted him to my arrival.

He walked to the credenza and filled both mugs. Back at the sofa, he handed me one and sat down at the end away from me, sipping at his coffee and, as usual, waiting for me to tell him what I needed. So, I filled him on the case, emphasizing the problem Heather and I had with finding information on Boulware.

"So, let me see if I have this straight," he said. "You have no problem with picking up this painting, but you're perplexed by Mr. Boulware being as the kids nowadays say . . . off the grid?"

"Yeah. I mean, I can't figure out how he can manage to be *completely* unrecorded."

"It's simple, Al, he's *not* unrecorded."

"Say What?"

He smiled at me. "I'm surprised you hadn't already figured this one out yourself, lad. Sure, the name Chester Boulware is pretty well hidden through using this blind trust as a cutout . . . and, that's actually pretty ingenious. But, somewhere, probably in the incorporation papers for Phoenix Corporation, is a name, and that name will be associated with a multitude of records, from social security number to tax records."

"I know that," I said. "That's why I have Heather trying to get the dirt on Phoenix."

"Good, but that will give you something important, that you don't seem to realize. It will give you Chester Boulware's real name."

He couldn't have shocked me more if he'd reached across the sofa and slapped me. Of course. And, he'd been right; I hadn't come to that conclusion. I'd been so focused on the forest I'd neglected to look carefully at the individual trees. But, as soon as he said it, it made perfect sense.

"I'll let Heather know so she can focus on that," I said.

"Good, now tell me more about this job of yours. Somehow, I never pictured you as a transporter."

I gave him a quick rundown, and showed him the photo of the painting. He took it and peered at it, frowning as he did so.

"What's the matter?"

"I don't know," he said. "There's something about this painting. It's right at the edge of my consciousness, but I can't recall." He shrugged. "Probably just some bit of trivia." He handed the photo back. "So, when do you pick it up?"

"As soon as Boulware gets word from the seller with the pick-up location."

"I guess I don't have to tell you to be cautious?"

"Of course you don't. Caution is my middle name. Besides, what could be dangerous about ferrying around three quarters of a million dollars and trading it for an obviously valuable painting, and doing it the way you spies used to trade secrets?"

He just smiled at me over the rim of his cup.

Chapter
Ten

I got home early and Sandra and I had a light supper, listened to classical music on NPR for a couple of hours and, after a little cuddling, went to sleep early. We both woke up around 5:30, completely refreshed, and did our morning run through the forest followed by a vigorous workout on the heavy bag in the barn behind the house. While she showered and got ready for school, I meditated, and then took my own shower while she started breakfast. I came down just as she was lining up four slices of bacon on a paper towel to soak up the grease. The aroma of freshly brewed coffee competed with the lilac-scented bath oil she'd used. One made me hungry, while the other made me horny, but I had to do the biscuits and scrambled eggs, so I just kissed her on the back of her neck and patted her beautifully formed backside.

"Hey, if you want breakfast, watch where you put your hands," she said, wiggling her butt at me.

"What if it's you I want for breakfast?"

She turned, laid a finger against her nose, and scrunched her eyes closed. "Nah, I think I'd rather have scrambled eggs and biscuits," she said. "Besides, wasn't last night enough for a while?"

"It was enough for last night, but today is a new day." I put the egg I was about to break down and moved over, pulling her into my arms. "Actually, I never get enough of you."

She ground her body against mine. "I never thought I'd be saying this, Al Pennyback," she said. "But, I feel the same way." She pulled back. "But, I have to get to school, and I'm famished—for food—so, we really have no time."

I knew that. But, it didn't make pulling away from her any easier. "Okay, eggs and biscuits coming up."

I broke four eggs into a medium sized bowl and whipped them thoroughly, then added salt, pepper, garlic powder, chopped green onions, chopped jalapeno peppers, and diced tomatoes. I set the mixture aside and mixed flour, salt, and baking powder in another medium bowl. I then cut some butter and vegetable oil into the flour mixture and mixed in a quarter cup of buttermilk and a quarter cup of cream. I stirred until the mixture was tacky, and then poured it onto a floured board and shaped it by hand into a quarter-inch-thick oval. I dipped a water glass into the flour and cut out ten three-inch diameter biscuits which I put on a pizza pan and into the preheated oven. While the biscuits cooked, I put a tablespoon of vegetable oil into my big iron skillet and put it on the stove to heat. I put two tablespoons of buttermilk into the egg mixture, mixed it up and poured it into the now steaming skillet. I stirred it around with a spatula while it cooked, ending up with a light yellow fluffy pile of eggs. I shoveled the eggs onto a platter and put the skillet in the sink. By now, the biscuits were light brown on top, so I turned off the oven but left them in to brown further while I put the eggs and bacon on two plates and put them on the table. Sandra poured two cups of coffee. The biscuits were just the right shade of brown when I took them out of the oven and put the pizza pan on top of an oven mitt in the center of the table.

"What would you like on your biscuits, babe, honey or jam?" I asked.

"Let's go wild and have both," she said, licking her lips.

So, we did, alternating between honey and grape jam. We finished every biscuit. Afterwards, with our second cups of coffee in hand, we sat back and rubbed our bellies. Now that my stomach was full, my mind was free to move on to something other than food, and of course, it roamed right onto the case, which caused me to frown.

"What's wrong, Al?" Sandra asked. She's sensitive to my moods. Hell, she's a high school teacher; she's sensitive to moods, period.

"It's this case I'm *not* working on. It's giving me fits."

She gave me the look that I'm sure she's perfected for students who are not making sense.

"How can a case you're not working on be bothering you?"

I told her. We'd been preoccupied with each other's bodies the night before, so I hadn't gotten around to talking to her about my new case. I often bounced ideas off her. Where Heather was the computer geek, Sandra had an insight into people, no doubt from her many years as a teacher. Sometimes, she was able to see something that both Heather and I'd missed. I gave her every detail about the case, including Heather's inability to find anything on our client.

"So," I said, raising my hands defensively. "While it might not sound like it makes sense, you see what I mean about *not* working on this case?"

She patted my hand.

"Of course I do, babe. But, Carlton's right, you know. It's impossible for anyone to be completely unrecorded in this country, so it's just a matter of Heather coming up with Chester Boulware's real name."

"I think this Phoenix Corporation's the key," I said. "If we can track it down, I've no doubt we'll discover his true identity."

"In the meantime, though, I'm really interested in this painting he wants you to retrieve."

"It's just a painting, and not a particularly good one at that," I said, shrugging.

"I doubt that." She laughed. "Three quarters of a million dollars is a lot of money for a painting that's not particularly good. Do you have a picture of it?"

I'd transferred the folded photo to my clean shirt when I dressed. I took it out and put it on the table. She picked it up and stared at it for several seconds. Then, her eyebrows started doing a little dance, bouncing up and down, and she pursed her lips and let out a whistle like a tea kettle coming to a boil.

"What is it?" I asked.

"Al, darling, you have to learn more about art." She placed the picture on the table and stabbed it with her index finger. "This black and white photo doesn't do this painting justice. It's not just *good*, it's great."

Art, I know, is subjective. One man's soup can is another man's art. I suppose, though, she was right. In black and white, the painting was unremarkable, but maybe it was a different picture in color.

"If you say so, but, I've seen better."

"It's not just that this is one of Vincent Van Gogh's more famous paintings," she said, correctly pronouncing the artist's name 'Gock'. "It's the history of this particular painting. You should be asking yourself why your client is being offered this painting, who is offering it to him, and how they came by it."

"Why?" I can be a bit dense sometimes.

"Because, this painting was supposed to have been destroyed when the Allies dropped bombs on the town of Magdeburg during World War Two, completely demolished the museum in which it was hanging."

Chapter
Eleven

Sandra was right. I needed to expand my circle of knowledge to encompass art. What she told me was mind-blowing, in both its details *and* its implications.

During my time in the army, I'd been exposed to military history, a lot of it about World War II, but that had mostly the most famous battles and the generals who led them. I hadn't paid much attention to the politics of the war, what few lectures I'd heard. Except for Roosevelt's difficulty getting the isolationist U.S. Congress and people to support Britain and the Soviet Union in their early efforts against the Nazi juggernaut, and the animus that developed when Eisenhower shoes Field Marshal Montgomery over American General George Patton to lead the final thrust into Germany after Normandy, little of the history interested me.

In college, one of Sandra's history professors had assigned Hitler's *Mein Kampf* as reading. As distasteful as it had been, it had made her curious about Hitler and his ability to pull the wool over an entire country's eyes so successfully.

"You know what P.T. Barnum said about 'one born every minute'," I said when she'd told me that. "Hitler and his minions were masters at telling people what they wanted to hear, and playing on their fears. In that way, they're not unlike some of our politicians."

"I suppose you're right," she said. "But, that wasn't what I was thinking about. You do know that Hitler was an artist, right?"

"No, I don't think I'd heard that one before."

"Well, he was. He failed, though, to get into one of Germany's prestigious art academies, which is beside the point. What is pertinent is that along with his master race theories and war against 'undesirables,' which included more than the Jews, he never lost his interest in art. During the time the Nazis were in charge of Germany, he attempted to purge what he termed 'degenerate' influences from art and literature. Impressionist artists like Van Gogh, and artists determined not to have Aryan blood, were considered degenerate, and their works were banned or destroyed, not just in Germany but in all the areas under Nazi control."

I nodded. "Yeah, many dictatorships try to manipulate people through art and books," I said. "You paint or write to the party line, or you suffer the consequences." Of course, leave it to the Nazis to add the element of race to the criteria.

"Few, though, were as systematic or as successful at it as the Nazis were. It's estimated that between 1937 and 1945 under Hitler, the Nazis looted over 750,000 valuable works of art. Many were burned or destroyed, but some were sold to the highest bidder, and the proceeds added to the Nazi war chest."

"Sort of like they did with the valuables they stripped from concentration camp victims."

"Exactly," she said. "And, that's where your painting comes into the picture."

"You mean this picture of some old guy walking down the road?"

"Not just *any* old guy. That picture is a self-portrait. It's called 'The Painter on the Road to Tarascon,' or "The Painter on His Way to Work,' and it's a rough color sketch of Van Gogh with boxes, props, and canvasses on a sunny road to his studio in Tarascon.

He painted it in 1888, and in the summer of that year, sent it to his brother Theo."

"How do you know so much about it?"

"When I was studying Hitler's background, I ran across references to stolen art, and happened to see a translation of Vincent's letter to Theo in an old book. It referenced the painting. The book in question was one about the Nazi art thefts. This painting, one of more than 2,000 known works of Van Gogh, is one of six thought to have been destroyed, most by the artist himself, but this one was in Nazi hands at the time of its reported destruction."

"Why *reported* destruction?"

"In 1945, this picture, along with hundreds of others that had been classified degenerate by the Nazi government, was reported to be in the Kaiser Friedrich Museum in Magdeburg, Germany. In January, 1945, the British air force carpet bombed the city, destroying nearly 90 percent of it, including the museum district, so the assumption was that this painting, too, was among the works destroyed."

My mind kicked into gear. I was beginning to see where she was going with her narrative. "There's a 'but' in there somewhere, though, right?"

"But, it could never be substantiated. The Nazis also kept looted art in a nearby salt mine, so it could have been there during the bombing raid," she said. "The U.S. Army occupied the city in April, 1945, but relinquished it to Soviet forces in July, and it became part of the Soviet zone of occupation, and subsequently East Germany, so no one was able to investigate it carefully."

"You think this 'Painter on His Way to Work' could have survived the bombing?"

She looked at the photo again. It was tightly cropped, showing an unframed canvas leaning against a chair. The background was in shadow, and there were no clues as to when the photo was taken, and since it was a reproduction of a photo, there was no way to know that it wasn't a photo of a photo.

"It could have, and if this job you're taking is for real, it *did*. Just think about it, Al. Suppose this painting was in the salt mine and not in the museum as once thought. Our troops wouldn't have been focusing on art when they entered Magdeburg, and they were only there three months. It was under Communist control from 1945 until East and West Germany were reunited in 1990. If it wasn't destroyed, it could be like the thousands of other missing paintings from the Nazi era, in some private collection."

"And, suddenly it comes to light, being offered to a recluse here in the United States, and a man who is something of an enigma himself."

This case got more interesting by the minute.

Charles Ray

Chapter
Twelve

The weekend passed quietly. Sandra and I went out to dinner at a Thai restaurant on Rockville Pike near White Flint Mall on Saturday, but spent the rest of the time just hanging around the house, dividing Sunday almost evenly between horseplay in the bedroom and workouts in the barn.

Monday came much too soon, and then the week did what weeks do when you're idle, it slowed to a crawl. Heather was moody because of her inability to find information on

Chester Boulware or Phoenix Corporation. Her mood wasn't improved by my telling her what I'd learned from Sandra about the painting. It was as if she felt that it was *her* job to discover these things, not someone else's. When she started researching the painting, and found an Internet site that described the Allied bombings of Magdeburg, her mood turned as dark as midnight without a moon. When she showed me the site describing the January 16, 1945 RAF bombing of the city, I understood.

While there was a synthetic fuel plant on the outskirts of the city, which the Americans and British were determined to destroy, the January raid was on the city itself, with concussion bombs taking the roofs off buildings which made it easier for the following incendiary bombs to ignite. To the crews of the RAF Lancaster Bombers, after the strike, the city must have looked like an orange carpet of fire. Over 90 percent of the structures were destroyed, and over 2,000 civilians were killed in that one raid alone. It didn't match the carnage of the Dresden raid, but considering the size of Magdeburg, it was devastating. Despite the destruction I'd seen during my time in the army, I couldn't even imagine what the first American soldiers entering the city in April 1945 must have seen or felt.

We were both feeling foul after that, so we just avoided each other. I know she wasn't mad at me or anything, or pissed because I'd been part of the military machine that would do such things, but there was no sense pushing my luck; I needed her to work her magic for me, and we'd been partners far too long to let ancient history, things that happened before either of was even born, to come between us.

On Wednesday, I remembered to call Raine and tell him what Sandra had told me about the painting.

"I thought I recognized that picture," he said. "So, your client is dealing in stolen art, and not just your garden variety stolen art, but the infamous Nazi stolen art. That might explain his use of an alias. There are some serious people trying to track that missing art, and they might not be too well disposed to someone trying to buy it under the table."

"Are we talking Israeli Nazi hunters here?"

"Not exactly . . . well, the Israelis are involved, but so are we, the Germans, the Russians, hell who knows how many other governments. And, that's just the official organizations. I imagine there are half a dozen criminal organizations in on the hunt as well."

"I guess that also explains why the sellers are being so cryptic and secretive. I'd think this painting would be worth a lot more than three quarters of a million, though."

"I'm sure it's worth considerably more," he said. "But, if the sellers need to move it quickly, they've probably priced it to move. It is stolen after all, so it's pretty much clear profit for them."

Even with all the unanswered questions, I felt I knew what I was dealing with.

Chapter
Thirteen

Thursday morning, just as I was dressing for my morning run, my phone rang. It was Quincy. I looked at my watch. It was 5:45. I knew that Quincy wasn't a morning person.

"Why are you calling me so early, Quincy?" I asked.

"Chester Boulware wants to see us," he said.

"Can't he wait until a decent hour?"

"What can I say, buddy, he doesn't call me often, but when he does, it's usually early in the morning."

I looked over at the bed. Sandra was awake, sort of, sitting up with the cover at her waist, looking bleary-eyed at me. It was nearly an hour earlier than I usually woke up, but something had jarred me awake, so I'd eased out of bed, trying not to wake her.

"What is it?" she asked in a mumbling voice full of sleep.

I put my hand over the mouthpiece. "Nothing, babe, go back to sleep."

She said something that sounded like 'Hmph' and dove beneath the covers. I went into the bathroom.

"Okay, Quincy," I said, as I closed the bathroom door. "What does he want with us at oh-dark-thirty? What's so important that it couldn't wait at least until I've had my breakfast?"

"He received the contact information and pick-up instructions," he replied, as if that explained it all. "Besides, he's inviting us to have breakfast with him."

"Quincy, you know I prefer eating breakfast at home."

"He also said he has your fee—your full fee—which he's prepared to pay in advance."

"Tell him I like my eggs scrambled."

I went back to the bedroom and started stripping off my running togs. Sandra peeked at me over the hem of the sheet.

"You coming back to bed?" she asked.

I walked over and kissed the top of her head. "No, you go on back to sleep, babe. I've got to meet a client, so I won't be here for breakfast. See you this evening."

She said 'hmph' again and buried her head in the pillow. Sandra gets up at 6:30 to run and work out with me, but she is not a 'before 6:00 am' person. I dressed as quietly as possible and tiptoed out of the bedroom.

I was on River Road heading for Boulware's place by 6:10. One of the things I got down pat during my time in the army was the 4-S morning. That's shit, shave, shower, and shine, and since I don't have to shine boots every day, the 3-S day is a snap. Traffic on River Road that early in the morning is barely a trickle compared to what it is by 6:45, so I was pulling up to the big iron gate just before 6:35.

The pad for guest parking was empty. I'd beaten Quincy there. The same guy opened the door for me.

"Mr. Pennyback. The master is waiting for you in the breakfast nook. Please follow me."

I followed him, going the opposite way from the way we'd gone on my first visit. There were as many paintings on the walls, and small to medium-sized statues and vases on the floor against the walls as I'd seen going in the opposite direction. Our journey ended in a sun room with one wall entirely of tinted glass looking out on a sculptured garden filled with topiary and statues similar to the front lawn.

Boulware, draped in a deep green robe with gold lapels, occupied one side of a small square table, seated so that he could look at the garden through the wall. As I entered, he motioned a meaty hand at the chair opposite him.

"Good morning, Mr. Pennyback. Thank you for agreeing to join me." I sat. He didn't offer to shake hands, which was fine with me. "I assume that you don't like to sit with your back to a door. I'm much the same. Quincy can have that honor." He was very perceptive. "What would you like for breakfast?"

My surprise that he'd read me that easily caused me to almost miss his question. I tried not to let it show by rubbing my hand across my jaw and furrowing my brow as if I was thinking on it.

"Uh, I'm your guest," I said. "So, I suppose I'll have whatever you're having." I was hoping he wasn't one of those people who favored Continental breakfasts, dry toast with overly sweet jam and bits of cheese didn't cut it for me.

"No, as my guest, you can have whatever pleases you." His lips quirked upwards and he regarded me through narrow slits.

Okay, I thought. Let's see if you really mean that. "I was planning to have sausage, scrambled eggs, hash browns and biscuits this morning," I said.

He smiled and nodded. "That sounds like a good substantial breakfast. Breakfast is the most important meal of the day, and it should be hearty. I approve.

He twisted around and lifted a phone from the cabinet behind him. After punching in a series of numbers he ordered for three, adding a rasher of bacon, honey, strawberry jam, and a fresh pot of coffee.

"Quincy loses the option of choosing," he said. "That'll teach him to be late for breakfast. While we wait, would you care for a cup of coffee? I've already had one, but I'm in the mood for another. I'm sure you'll like it. It's made from freshly-ground Colombian beans."

"Sounds fine to me." When he lifted the carafe from the shelf where it sat near the phone, the aroma *smelled* fine too.

He poured two cups, and slid one across the table to me. "No sugar or cream if I recall," he said. "I sometimes like a bit of sugar and a lot of cream in mine." And, he proceeded to pour enough cream into the cup to change the dark brown liquid to the color of chocolate milk without too much chocolate. Then he stirred in three teaspoons of sugar.

"I don't like to have anything get between me and the taste of my coffee," I said, and took a sip. Except for the lack of chicory, it was every bit as good as Raine's. I sighed with contentment.

We silently sipped our coffee for the next twenty minutes. An enigma he might be, but Boulware was beginning to impress me. Not too many people can go for such a long period of silence without succumbing to the urge to fill the void with noise. Like me, though, he seemed content to sit in silence and enjoy his coffee.

Our solitude was broken by the butler . . . I wasn't sure what his actual title was, or if, even, he was the only one in the house, but he dressed, acted, and talked like my image of a butler . . . came in behind a long, wheeled trolley upon which were three large dinner plates, a large silver urn, and several covered white containers which I assumed were the condiments Boulware had ordered. Silently, he put a plate in front of each of us, the third to my right, which would have Quincy facing the wall, and then arranged the urn and condiment containers in the center of the table. From a shelf underneath the trolley, he took out three linen napkins and placed them beside each plate, followed by knives, spoons, and forks. When things were arranged to his apparent satisfaction, he silently withdrew.

Moments later, before we could even put our napkins in our laps, he was back at the door with Quincy beside him.

"Sorry I'm late," Quincy said. He came in and sat in the chair with his back to the door. "Traffic was heavy coming out of the

District."

"Not to worry," Boulware said. "The food was just served, so, in fact, you're right on time. Shall we eat, gentlemen?"

For a few minutes we ate in relative silence, the only sounds the light scraping of utensils on the plates. I had to admit that the food was as good as I could have cooked myself—better when I considered that I *hadn't* had to cook it.

When our plates were clean, and we were having our second coffee, the butler appeared and silently cleared the table. I hadn't seen Boulware reach behind him, but there had to be some way he had of signaling the man. More pieces of the puzzle that was there, lurking in the back of my mind the entire time. I decided to let Boulware take the lead. No sense letting him know that at the moment he was more of the focus of my thoughts than the job he'd hired me to do.

He took a sip from his cup, wiped his lips with the napkin, and leaned back.

"Now, gentlemen, the reason I requested your presence this morning," he said. "I have received the location and final instructions for delivery of the painting."

With some effort, he leaned to the side. I worried that his bulk would cause him to continue tipping over, and I wasn't sure that Quincy and I together would be able to lift him back up, but he managed to reach down and get a black stiff briefcase that was beside his chair. He pushed his cup aside and put it on the table. Carefully he thumbed open the two latches and opened it, then turned it so that I could see inside.

Neat stacks of hundred dollar bills lined the briefcase. A single sheet of paper lay atop the cash. Boulware picked the paper up and passed it to me.

"This paper contains the directions to the exchange location," he said. "The money in the briefcase is your fee. You may count it if you wish, but there are one hundred stacks of hundred dollar bills, the entire fee in advance."

"What about the money to pay for the painting?" I asked.

He pointed to the corner behind me. A large green canvas bag, about three feet high by four feet wide, bulging a bit at the bottom, sat against the wall in the far corner of the room. I'd not noticed it when I came in.

"The entire amount, in banded hundred dollar bills, is in that case," he said. "You can also use it to transport the painting back here."

I nodded and picked the paper up. It was plain bond paper, lacking any kind of identifying marks, and the printing on it looked like it had been run through a garden variety computer printer. It was brief and to the point. On Saturday, March 15, at 8:00 am, I was to be at the intersection of state roads 135 and 495, northeast of Oakland, the county seat of Garrett County, the westernmost county in Maryland. There was a local park near the intersection, and I was to pull my car into a parking space as near to the entrance as possible, get out, and stand in front of the car with a folded newspaper under my right arm.

I hadn't expected such a cloak and dagger routine, but I know nothing about the art business, legitimate or otherwise, so I assumed this was standard protocol. I folded the paper and put it into my shirt pocket. Then, I got up and walked to the corner. I grabbed the thick strap and hefted the bag from the floor. Want to know something interesting? Three quarters of a million dollars, even in hundred dollar bills, is heavy.

"Heavy," I said as I let the bag drop to the floor.

"Yes, quite," Boulware said. "Will that be a problem?"

"No, no problem at all. Can you get your man to haul it out to my car for me?" While he dialed the phone, I carefully closed and picked up the briefcase containing my fee. I used the pads of my thumbs to close the lid, and my knuckles to snap the locks. Then, I hooked my index and second finger in the grip, resting the weight of the case between the joints. That way, there was less chance of me accidentally smudging Boulware's fingerprints. After removing the money from the case, I planned to pass it to Buster, so he could have his crime lab guys dust it, lift Boulware's prints, and run them through every data base they could think of. I was determined to know Chester Boulware's true identity.

Chapter
Fourteen

Once I had the large case full of money stuffed into the back seat of my Volkswagen and the briefcase with my fee on the passenger seat beside me, I assured Boulware that I would make the rendezvous and get his painting, and then drove straight to the office.

I gave Heather the instructions so that she could map out a driving route and called Buster to come and pick up the briefcase to dust for Boulware's fingerprints. This was after Heather and I had carefully opened it, using surgical gloves from a box in the bottom drawer of her desk—one of her 'you never know when you'll need them' purchases—and removed the hundred grand, which she put in a three large manila envelopes and stashed in the bottom drawer of her desk for safekeeping until her lunch hour when she took them to the bank near the Waterfront Metro Station and deposited the money into our account.

Buster didn't show up to get the briefcase until the middle of the afternoon, and he wasn't in the best of moods.

"You know, bro, I got other cases to work on," he grumbled as soon as he walked through the door.

"We know," Heather said, batting her eye lashes at him. "But, this is important, or we wouldn't ask. It's just a little fingerprint check."

Buster's married, and Alma, who is half his size, would kill him if he made a play for another woman, but for some reason, she never minded his flirtation with Heather.

"Well, I'll do it for you, Heather. Anything for you." He smiled at her, and tossed a frown my way. "I can get the lab boys to dust it today, but it'll have to go into the queue. IAFIS gets over 60 million requests a year from ever cop shop in the country, and they turn 'em around pretty fast, but we're just one of many. Hell, it'll take my guys at least a day to do the request."

I understood the situation. The FBI's Integrated Automated Fingerprint Identification System, or IAFIS, was a computer system containing over 100 million prints. It operated 24/7, and could respond to an ID request in half an hour if it was related to a crime. Ours was a routine civilian request that as far as we knew didn't involve a crime, so that could take over an hour for the system to respond to. It was still better than the old system in place before 1999, which required manual searches of the files and could take days.

"Don't forget to check Interpol," Heather said.

"What's Interpol got to do with this?" Buster asked.

"Just a hunch," she responded. "Al did tell you about the art link, right?"

"Uh, yeah."

"Well, stolen European art, possible European connection, Interpol."

She gave him her best 'aren't I smart' look, while he could only stare back, slack jawed. Heather's not just a computer expert, she's turning into a first-rate detective.

"Okay, but that's just gonna take longer."

"Better slow than we miss something."

He made a snorting sound, but accepted a pair of her surgical gloves to carry the case away.

"Interpol, that was good thinking," I said after he'd gone.

"It's what we get paid for," she said, and turned back to whatever she was doing on her computer.

I was effectively dismissed, so I went to my office and spent the rest of the afternoon playing chess.

I didn't win a single game.

Chapter
Fifteen

Other than being trounced by the computer at chess, the rest of my Thursday was uneventful. Actually, there was nothing particularly eventful about that, since it happened so frequently. I took the money-filled canvas bag home with me, and arranged for Heather to pick me up on Friday morning and drive me to an Enterprise dealer in Germantown where I rented a silver Toyota

4-Runner. I chose the big SUV, because I wasn't sure what kind of roads I might have to drive over in western Maryland—a mostly rural area according to Heather's early research—and, it had more space for carrying things than my little bug. The main reason, though, was that the last time I drove my own car into an unfamiliar rural area, a militia asshole had blown it up with a rocket propelled grenade. I took full insurance on the rental just to be on the safe side.

Back at the office, she showed me the map and route information she'd printed out. The distance from DC to the rendezvous point was just a bit under 190 miles, and most of it was by way of interstate highways. The final 50 miles or so, though, were state highways, and through the mountains. If I decided to leave home on Saturday, I'd have to depart my house before 4:00 a.m., so I decided to drive up on Friday afternoon and find a motel room as close to the rendezvous as possible. With a hundred grand fee, the car rental and motel cost wouldn't even make a dent. It did mean, though, that I'd miss my Friday evening with Sandra. When I got home that evening and told her my plans, she had the perfect solution—we did our Friday night out on Thursday instead.

Since I wasn't planning to go to the office, I let Sandra sleep in until 6:40 Friday morning. After I rousted her, we changed and went for a run and a workout. I meditated, and then followed her into the shower, catching the last few minutes, which allowed some horseplay. Then, I finished showering while she dressed. We cooked breakfast together, and took our time eating it, savoring the time together. I promised her that I'd get back as soon as I could on Saturday after picking up and delivering the painting to Boulware, and then we'd have the rest of the weekend to ourselves.

We clung to each other for a long time after breakfast, and I stood on the porch and watched her drive off to school, and stayed there for a long time after her car was out of view.

I took my time cleaning the kitchen, scrubbing every surface twice until it glistened. Satisfied that there was nothing I'd missed, I went into the bedroom to pack.

Normally, when I travel for business, it's either dress for meeting people; a pair of dress pants, one long-sleeved shirt, and a jacket; or for not being seen; which meant black cotton trousers, black sweater and ski mask. For this one, though, I couldn't make up my mind. I couldn't see people choosing to meet in a rural area like western Maryland as the coat and tie type, but I shouldn't have to do any kind of recon. I wasn't sure if the meeting would be outdoors or indoors either, and even though the weather in DC was getting warmer during the day, I figured it would be cooler in the mountains.

So, I compromised. I threw one pair of black pants, the ones with pockets on the legs, into my old beat up backpack, along with a black cotton shirt, long-sleeved just in case. Then, I added a pair of khakis, two brown cotton shirts, one long-sleeved and one short-sleeved, underwear for two nights, and an extra pair of socks. I decided to take just one set of footwear, my canvas-sided black recce boots with the rippled leather soles. With my pant legs over them, they don't look too bad, and their comfortable for driving as well as walking. It also meant I wouldn't have the weight of extra shoes. There was a coil of quarter-inch rope in the bottom of the backpack. I'd had need of it on an earlier job and had left it there just to keep it from getting tangled with other junk in my closet. I briefly considered taking it out. It didn't weigh much, though, so I just left it.

I threw the backpack on the bed and dressed in a pair of light khaki pants and a short-sleeved beige cotton shirt, and pulled a light green windbreaker from the closet.

The last item I took from the closet was my K-Bar knife. I didn't think I'd need it, but it felt comfortable having it. I tossed it into the backpack and tied it shut.

I put the backpack into the back seat of the 4-Runner, and then put the case with Boulware's money in beside it. Heather's directions went on the passenger seat along with two quart bottles of Poland Spring water. I was ready for the road by 10:00 a.m.

Traffic on I-270 north was light, mostly trucks heading to Pennsylvania and points north and west, so I made good time to the I-70 interchange in Frederick. There were more trucks on I-70 west, which is the main interstate between Baltimore and Pittsburgh. The terrain from Frederick, north and west, is more mountainous, with stunning views of neat farms and forests as you top hills. A few miles past Hagerstown I saw signs for Hancock, where I picked up I-68 west toward West Virginia. It was like I'd entered a different country. The sliver of Maryland that juts west, sandwiched between West Virginia to the south and Pennsylvania to the north, it's almost entirely agricultural or forest land. The few small towns are nestled in little valleys, where little can be seen beyond the occasional church steeple. The traffic from Hagerstown was a mixed lot; a few cars and lots of semis mixed in with farm machinery, causing me to drop my speed to around 50 mph. As a result of the slower speed, it was 3:50 when I reached the exit at Grantsville, which was where I'd planned to spend the night. There was a Comfort Inn right at the exit, and luckily they had a ground floor vacancy located so that I could keep an eye on my vehicle. I hauled the money case and my backpack into the room, and after taking a shower, lay back on the bed and watched afternoon shows on the room's TV.

Just before dark, I got directions to a Burger King from the desk clerk, went out and got myself a burger, fries and a large Fanta orange and took them back to the room. I flipped channels while I ate, and at 7:30 I muted the sound and called Sandra.

"How is the trip so far?" she asked.

"The mountains were beautiful for the first thirty minutes, but they get boring after that."

"I wish I was with you."

"I wish you were here," I said. "There's absolutely nothing to do until morning."

"I could talk dirty to you on the phone," she offered.

"Don't you dare! I need to get some sleep tonight, not lay awake thinking about what I'm missing."

"In that case, I should let you go, or I won't be able to sleep."

"Sleep tight, babe, and don't let the bed bugs bite."

"You too, Al . . . I love you."

"I love you, too, babe."

"Hang up," she said.

"No, you hang up."

"You called, so you're the one who is supposed to hang up."

I have no idea where that little bit of nonsense came from, but it made me feel better.

"Okay," I said. "I'll make you a deal . . . I'll

count to three, and we'll both hang up at the same time."

"Is that on three or after three?"

"On three . . . ready . . . one . . . two . . . three." I broke the connection without waiting to see if she did as well.

I lay there on the bed for another three hours with the TV on, but paying no attention to what was on the screen. It was mostly nonsense anyway. At 10:30 I used the remote to turn it off, turned off the room lights, and crawled under the covers. I was asleep almost as soon as my head snuggled into the pillow.

Charles Ray

Chapter
Sixteen

The sun's rays coming through a gap in the curtains woke me at 5:30 the next morning. I'd slept the night through, and if I dreamed, I didn't remember doing so.

After a shower and shave, I put on my black cargo pants and shirt, strapped my K-Bar to my right ankle, and took my backpack to the 4-Runner. I went back to the room and retrieved the heavier canvas case which I took with me to the tiny dining room where they served a free breakfast of biscuits, do-it-yourself pancakes, boiled eggs and slightly greasy bacon. I washed everything down with coffee from a large machine. It was drinkable, but definitely not Jamaican or Colombian. I finished breakfast and checked out at 6:40. By 6:45, I was on the road.

From the on-ramp to I-68 to the State Road 495 exit was a few miles and with no traffic only took a few minutes. The little town of Grantsville was to the north, and in the morning mist the few low buildings near the interchange were like ghost houses. I didn't see anything higher than two floors.

South of I-68, it was mostly forest, farmland, scattered houses, a strip mall or two, and a quarry of some kind. The two-lane road wound lazily through the forests and thankfully I didn't encounter any farm vehicles before the fig lifted around 7:15.

By 8:00 I began to encounter more settlement. More housing developments, several paved roads intersecting with 495, and more churches. There was a bit of confusion when I saw signs for Swanton and came to a T intersection. I had to pull over and consult Heather's directions to find out that at this point, 495 was the right turn, which became Swanton Road, and was very near my destination. The rendezvous point was not at the intersection of 495 and State Road 135 as had been indicated, but was a mile farther west, on 135, and consisted of just a gravel-covered space big enough for three or four cars with a rusty trash barrel at one end, and the stake for a sign that had been removed. At least, I hoped it was the correct space. But, there was nothing else along the road resembling a park or parking area, just driveways to private residences, so I pulled in, angled the 4-Runner nose out, got out and leaned against the hood. I looked at my watch. 8:20. The fog had lifted and I could see clearly in both directions. Traffic was beginning to pick up, but no one seemed to pay me any attention.

So, I waited. And, I waited some more.

At 9:20, just when I was about to conclude that I was in the wrong location, a blue Ford F150 pickup with double cab and roll bar, and coming from the west, pulled off the road and stopped about twenty feet from me. Two guys got out. The driver was about my height, about one-sixty, with a narrow face, lank brown hair that flopped over his forehead, and mean looking brown eyes. He kept his hands in the pockets of his brown cargo pants and his eyes on me. The passenger was something else entirely. He was at least six-two, with the broad shoulders and large upper arms of a weight lifter. His square head was covered with yellowish-brown hair cut close. Piercing blue eyes sunken under a broad brow scanned me, my vehicle, and the surroundings as he approached me. He had a slight Nordic look to him. He kept his hands at his side, relaxed, but ready. I could see the bulge of a small handgun in the pocket of his pants which were identical to his companion's. In fact, with the brown cargo pants and brown shirts with military-style epaulets, they looked like members of some militia.

My muscles tensed, but I kept a calm expression on my face. I didn't see any sign of hostile intent, and couldn't do anything until they were both within kicking range anyway.

I looked at my watch. "You the guys with the painting? You're late," I said. I pointedly looked at my watch.

They stopped about six feet from me—too far to punch or kick—with the driver a pace or two behind the big guy.

"Yeah, you got the money?" the big guy said, ignoring my comment about the time. He spoke with a faint, unidentifiable accent.

"I have it."

"Let me see."

"Let me see the painting," I said.

He folded his arms across a massive chest. "I don't see that you have the money, you will not see the painting."

I couldn't argue with that. I'd probably do the same thing if our roles were reversed. At the same time, I had to maintain at least a small degree of control. "Okay, you can look, but not touch," I said.

He stood, still as a boulder, and stared at

me. I stared back. I'd been there before. I wasn't sure which army, but the guy was military or ex-military. I could tell by his bearing and haircut, but most of all, I could tell by his expression. And, I could also tell that he'd made me as well. We were like two old gray back gorillas, staring each other down to determine which was the alpha male We were cataloging each other's assets, assessing potential fighting skill, looking for possible weak points, and I was hoping like hell it wouldn't come to a confrontation, because I didn't see any weak points.

"That will be acceptable," he said finally.

I walked around the 4-Runner to the driver's side and opened the back door. Reaching in, I opened the case and stepped aside. He moved up to the door, never taking his eyes off me. Gingerly pushing aside the flap with one hand, he peered into the case. Finally, he stepped away from the car and nodded.

"Is fine. You follow us."

Charles Ray

Chapter
Seventeen

They drove back the way they came, keeping well within the speed limit. I followed, about four car lengths back. As we neared the town of Oakland the traffic picked up, so I closed to two car lengths, and then, to keep from losing sight of them, pulled up to within a few feet of the pickup's tailgate. If it bothered them, they didn't show it. The truck kept the same sedate speed.

Oakland was not unlike many other small Maryland towns I'd driven through, though spread out a bit more. The street we were on was lined with a mixture of residential properties, stores and what looked like government buildings. People, most wearing overalls or work garments, walked purposefully along the sidewalks, paying us no mind.

At a place where Route 135 turned sharply to the right, I saw a sign indicating one of the official looking buildings on my right was a District Court. A number of Maryland State Police and Garrett County Sheriff vehicles were in the parking lot, so I guessed that the cop house was located in close proximity to the court building.

The pickup didn't make the turn. Instead, he kept going straight. The sign at the corner identified the new direction as E. Oak Street, which turned out to be a winding two-lane road through a residential area at first, and then was flanked by a forest, with one or two homes set on wooded lots on the right side. We made a sharp right, then a left, and were soon on a paved road that wound through a thick forest. The trees grew right up to the gravel shoulder, and I saw no sign of agriculture or residences on either side. The pickup speeded up. I pressed the gas to keep up, and soon we were zipping along at a hair-raising 50 mph, with me hoping we wouldn't come around a curve and plow into a tractor or slow-moving truck.

After thirty minutes, the pickup's left

signal light started blinking, and slowed. Then, it turned left onto a dirt road that I would have passed without seeing, and we started going uphill. Other than a few bumps, the road appeared well maintained. The pickup, though, kicked up a cloud of red dust that made it hard to see. I eased off on the gas pedal to allow a bit more distance, because the driver was still doing almost fifty. The sun was high in the sky, but the towering trees, growing close together, cast a shadow over the road which, along with the dust cloud, created a twilight effect.

I felt a tingling sensation at the back of my neck. Part of it was from the fact that I had no idea where I was, and part was . . . just a feeling of unease, like the unease I'd often felt when on a combat patrol as we neared the objective area. Despite all the briefings, we never really knew what would be waiting for us. And, this time, I was entering the objective area without benefit of a briefing.

I was so focused on my feeling of unease, I almost missed it when the pickup turned left off the dirt road we were on to another unmarked dirt road that was little more than tire tracks worn down by the passage of many vehicles. A strip of dusty grass grew between the tracks. The 4-Runner skidded a bit as I whipped the wheel left to make the turn, but stayed on the road.

The hard-packed clay track was bumpy and not at all well-maintained, but the pickup didn't kick up as much dust, so I closed the gap between us, hanging a car's length back. My gut told me we wouldn't be encountering any farm vehicles on this road.

The two sentries, one on each side of the road, appeared without warning. Two men, wearing camouflaged uniforms and carrying AR-15s, stepped out into the road from the trees and held their hands up for us to stop. I stomped the brakes and came to a bone-jarring halt inches from the back of the pickup.

One of the sentries walked over to the passenger side of the pickup and said something I couldn't hear. He nodded and glared back at me, and then he and his comrade stepped back into the trees. The pickup eased forward. Feeling the prickling sensation of being watched, I followed.

About fifty yards in front of the pickup I could see an arch of brightness. We were coming, if not out of the forest, at least to some kind of clearing. Shortly after entering the clearing, the pickup turned right and was out of view. As I came out of the shade of the trees whose branches arched over the road, I craned my neck to see where the pickup was. What I saw caused my mouth to gape open.

Ahead of me, the pickup pulled into an area about fifty feet wide and fifty yards deep, a rectangular, gravel-covered area that was being used as a parking lot. There were eight pickups and six 4-Runners, mostly in silver and blue, but two of the 4-Runners and three of the pickups were painted in a green and black camouflage pattern. Beyond the parking lot were three green and black camouflage-painted Quonset huts of the kind I hadn't seen since the army. To the left, a straight line from where we'd exited the forest, was a one-story log cabin with a parabolic antenna and several metal rod antennas on the roof, and left of that an area of patchy grass where a group of twenty men in cammie pants and green tee shirts were doing jumping jacks under the watchful eye of a mountain of a man with a bushy black beard and a voice I could hear even with the windows closed and from almost fifty yards away. I noticed AR-15s and AK-47s neatly stacked nearby. The clearing was surrounded on all sides by towering trees.

This location could only be seen by someone approaching on the road, and they would be stopped by the sentries before getting close enough to see anything, or from directly overhead. I wondered if this bunch had shoulder-fired surface-to-air missiles. They looked like they were ready for war, so it wouldn't have surprised me.

It didn't increase my level of comfort either.

The big guy got out of the pickup and walked back to me. He signaled for me to roll my window down.

"You go to the cabin," he said, pointing at the building with the antenna farm.

I got out and opened the back door to retrieve the money.

"You can leave it here," he said. "No one bother it."

"Thanks, but I'd feel better keeping it with me," I said as I hefted the heavy bag out and draped it over my shoulder. "No offense."

He just shrugged and turned on his heels, heading toward the cabin. I hitched up my load and followed; glad I didn't have to go too far. Seven hundred and fifty grand worth of hundred dollar bills is heavy.

A group of camouflaged men stood off to the right of the cabin. Their floppy campaign hats shaded their eyes, but the malevolent glares they shot my way were easy to see.

The big guy stopped at the door and knocked.

"Come in," a muffled and heavily accented voice said from the other side of the door.

Big guy opened the door and stepped to the side, motioning me to enter. As I walked past him, I saw a flicker of something in his eyes. If he hadn't been so big and tough looking I would have sworn it was fear.

Chapter
Eighteen

The room was sparsely furnished. There was just the one door. Two windows were set in the wall to the right and a door was in the wall on the left. A simple wooden desk sat facing the door. On the desk was a handheld two-way radio. With all the trees around, I figure one of the men in the pickup must have radioed in when we were about two miles out, which is about the maximum range you can get with even the devices with long antennas in wooded terrain. Two plain wooden chairs sat in front of it. Off to the right, two olive green ammunition cases were against the unfinished wall. Behind the desk was another wooden chair, identical to the two in front. A man sat in the chair. He didn't look particular imposing. His sandy hair was thinning and combed straight back over an egg-shaped head and I could see his pink scalp. He looked to be ten or fifteen pounds lighter than me, with rounded shoulders and a sunken chest. His head was down as he looked at a flimsy sheet paper he held in his gnarled, liver-spotted hands. He didn't look particularly frightening until he lifted his head and looked at me. I was reminded of Friederich Nietzsche's quote, "and, if thou gaze long into an abyss, the abyss will gaze long into thee." I felt like I was being bored into by a laser. The man's two dark eyes were as soulless as I've ever seen, and in my time, I've seen a lot of evil people.

He motioned toward the chair on the right.

"You have come with the money for the painting."

I took my time crossing the room, and sat in the indicated chair. I took the canvas case off my shoulder and leaned it against the back leg, but kept my hand on it.

"I have. My name's Al Pennyback and I work for Mr. Boulware's lawyer," I said. "May I see the painting?"

If he wanted to skip the pleasantries and get right down to business, that was fine with me.

"Why did . . . Boulware not come himself?"

How that was pertinent wasn't clear, but the tone of his voice *was*. He'd been expecting Boulware himself to come.

"Have you ever met Chester Boulware in person?" I asked.

His broad forehead wrinkled and a muscle under his left eye twitched. "That does not answer my question, but no, I have not met him in person."

"Well, if you had, you wouldn't ask such a question. Boulware's not exactly what I would call the moving around type."

He looked confused. Confused, and not a little angry.

"Please explain."

"The man's at least three hundred pounds, and not much of it's muscle. To get here, he'd have to be carried in the bed of a truck."

He leaned back in the chair and closed his eyes. His lips moved, but no sounds came out. When his eyes snapped open, he was again staring at me with that soulless look. I suddenly felt cold.

"That, unfortunately, changes things."

I definitely didn't like the way *that* sounded.

"Changes things? How?"

"I prefer dealing directly with . . . clients."

"I suppose I can understand that, but

what's the difference as long as you get your money?"

He stood, slowly, still staring at me like a cobra preparing to strike.

"I do not like changing my methods, not even to satisfy a wealthy client like this Boulware. You will tell him that."

What the hell, I thought. If the guy wanted to play hard ball with Boulware, that was between them. I wasn't refunding the one hundred grand. I took out my phone. There was no reception.

"Well now, that's gonna be a problem," I said. "Do you have a landline here I could use?"

"A . . . ah, yes, a telephone. Alas, I am afraid we do not, and mobile phones do not work up here."

"How were you able to contact Boulware?" I asked. "To make the offer and to send the instructions?"

I didn't believe him about the place not having a phone. It was a pretty good bet that the survivalist types I saw drilling outside were from the area and that this was their headquarters. With no cell coverage and just their rinky dink little walkie talkies, they were sure to have a method of communicating. Just not in this room. But, the room took up less than half the width of the building, and I figured the door on the left led to a room that had a phone. For some reason, this guy didn't want me knowing that.

"That is really not your concern."

"It is, but I won't argue the point. Okay, I'll relay your message to Boulware, but that means I'll have to go back to Oakland, or at least go somewhere that I have cell coverage," I said. "He won't be happy. You mind at least telling me your name, so he'll know I'm not jerking him around?"

He looked hesitant. Then, he shrugged and smiled. The smile didn't reach his eyes.

"I suppose it won't matter really. My name is Wesley Hendrik. Is that sufficient?"

It would have been if it had been my intent to make that call. But, as soon as he gave me his name, I decided that what I *was* going to do was get the hell out of Dodge. I'd been listening to the guy talk, and had finally judged his accent to be slightly Slavic, probably Russian. I've had some experience with Russian gangsters, none if it pleasant. There was no way this guy's birth certificate, the real one, had the name Wesley Hendrik on it. Probably Ivan or Vladimir, and who the hell knows what surname. I also realized that the big Slavic looking guy in the pickup had also had a hint of a Russian accent. How they got hooked up with a bunch of local militia yokels I didn't know, and I didn't want to know. All I wanted to do was put as much distance between me and them as possible.

"Yeah, that'll do it." I stood and hefted the case to my shoulder. His face stiffened when I did that. "I'm taking this with me, you understand, until we get the details ironed out."

He smiled. Again, the smile didn't reach those dark eyes. "Yes, I suppose that would be . . . prudent."

I backed slowly to the door. He just stood there and watched me go, those dark eyes boring into me.

The big guy was standing just outside the door.

"Where are you going?" he asked.

"I need to drive back down the road until I can get cell coverage," I said. "I need to make a phone call before we can conclude our business."

He looked confused, but made no move to restrain me. I walked slowly to my vehicle and after unlocking it stowed the case in the back seat. As I got behind the wheel I noticed the big guy going into the cabin. The men standing near the cabin were still eying me. I started the engine, put it in Drive and turned sharply and headed for the road. Just as I made the turn onto the road I glanced into the rearview mirror. I saw the big guy come running out of the cabin waving his arms and pointing my way. The men scrambled toward one of the Quonset huts, while he stood there with his hand on his hips glaring at me until the dust cloud the 4-Runner kicked up hid him from my view.

I didn't need a printed program to know

what was going on. Hendriks, or whatever his real name was, was sending them after me, probably to take the money, while keeping the painting to sell to some other sucker. That was probably his intent all along, except he'd expected Boulware to show up.

I wondered why he didn't just have them shoot me while I was there. A lot of questions were running through my mind, but no answers.

First things first, though. I had to get out of that damned forest and back to Oakland.

I was up the proverbial creek, though. In a leaky boat and without a paddle. If I slowed down, they were on me. If I kept going at my current rate of speed, I'd soon run out of gas, and they were on me, and it was becoming apparent that I didn't have enough gas to get to the end of the first dirt road and onto the other, much less make it to the highway and the safety of town.

My options were . . . nil.

Then, I saw something I hadn't noticed on the drive in. The trees to either side of the road here were not quite as thick or closely spaced as they'd been on the first road, and there was no ditch alongside. This truly was a route that had been beaten down by vehicles, probably the militia that owned the compound. It also had more twists and turns than a sidewinder rattlesnake crawling through the desert.

That gave me an idea.

I waited until I'd just entered one of what I recalled was a long series of S-curves, and the first curve was particularly long. What was even more important, the trees on the left were widely spaced, more than enough room for the 4-Runner. I counted "One-Mississippi, two-Mississippi, three-Mississippi," and jerked the wheel left. The 4-Runner fishtailed, and then straightened, and shot into the forest, barely missing a gnarled old oak. Luck was with me. Not only had I managed to miss the trees, but that side of the road was on the downslope, and very quickly, I could see through the rearview mirrors that I was well below the road's elevation.

The engine made a few sputtering sounds and died, but gravity and centrifugal force kept me moving. I maneuvered it toward a large clump of bushes, managing to get behind it before coming to a stop.

For a few seconds I just sat there with my head resting on the steering wheel. But, only for a few seconds.

At the speed they were driving, my pursuers might pass the spot where I turned off the road without noticing, but it wouldn't take them long to realize that I was no longer in front of them.

Chapter
Nineteen

Fear does strange things to you. When confronted with a frightening situation, the body has a fight or flight response. Normally, my response is to fight, unless the odds are stacked against me. Nearly two dozen heavily armed men and me with just my trusty K-Bar knife—those odds were stacked damned high, and not in my favor, so my response was flight.

I'd been nervous about the speed we'd been driving when we came up the road. Now, as I looked in my rearview mirror and saw the dust cloud of at least one pickup through the cloud my own vehicle was making, I pushed the gas pedal to the floor and hung onto the steering wheel like a drowning man clutching a life vest, hoping a deer didn't jump into the road in front of me.

Then, I glanced down at the dashboard. The needle on the gas gauge was almost all the way to the left. Damn, I was probably running on fumes. I'd filled the tank in Hagerstown, so there should have been at least half a tank left. Someone must have drained the tank while I was talking to Hendriks.

The odds against me were getting higher.

On the drive up, I'd been worried about the speed we'd been driving, but with at least one truckload of guys, no doubt armed to the teeth, on my tail, I threw caution to the wind and floored the 4-Runner.

Of course, that presented another problem. If I slowed down, they'd get me. But, based on the position of the needle, I was running on fumes, so when I ran out of gas, which I was likely to do before even getting to the main dirt road, they'd get me then as well.

I prayed silently that a horny Whitetail buck wouldn't jump into the road in front of me, and gripped the steering wheel tightly, while still jamming the gas pedal to the floor.

The road we were on twisted and turned like a snake, and at every turn I lost sight of my pursuers for several seconds. I also noticed that, unlike the main dirt road, the trees alongside me were more widely spaced, and that the track didn't have a ditch, but instead was level with the adjacent terrain. That gave me an idea, and a glimmer of hope.

When I entered the turn that I recalled was a triple-S and quite long, I kept my eyes peeled for an opening. Halfway through the second turn, I saw it; a space between the trees more than wide enough to accommodate the SUV.

I whipped the wheel left, causing the 4-Runner to fishtail, but I was able to get it straightened out, just in time to avoid slamming into a large tree on my right side. I kept going straight, checking the rearview mirrors until I could no longer see the road, which was uphill now, at a higher elevation than my vehicle. I then turned right and let up off the gas, allowing the weight of the vehicle, gravity, and centrifugal force to keep me moving.

I saw a large clump of bushes, about twenty feet across, and twelve feet high, and aimed for the downhill side of it. When I was even with the bushes, I slammed the brakes, coming to a bone-jarring stop. The engine made a clicking sound and a kind of sigh and then was silent. I turned the key to the 'off' position. It wasn't starting again until I refueled it, but I saw no sense in draining the battery.

For several seconds, I sat there with my forehead against the steering wheel, to allow my breathing to return to normal.

I was too far from the road to hear the sound of their engines, but, if they spotted my turn and came after me, I'd hear them soon enough.

When I didn't hear anything after thirty seconds, I got out and took the money from the back seat.

At the speed they were driving, it was a good chance they didn't notice the tire tracks leaving the road, but it wouldn't take them long to realize that I was no longer in front of them. Once they saw where I left the road, it was just a matter of minutes before they would find the 4-Runner, so I had to move fast.

Hoisting the case on my shoulder, I moved a bit farther downhill and then headed south, not bothering to try and conceal my tracks. After about two hundred yards, I stepped onto a hummock of grass and then, careful about where I stepped, I moved back uphill. I found a little copse of trees that were in full leaf and growing close to the ground. I pushed my way into the center of the copse and used my hands to scoop out a depression big enough to accommodate the case. After putting it in, I scraped dirt and leaves over it, smoothing the area as much as

I could to remove all signs of disturbance. After I was satisfied that my hiding place would withstand all but the most careful scrutiny, I carefully made my way out of the trees, and retraced my steps back to the hummock.

To keep them on the wrong trail for as long as possible, I stepped back onto my original trail and walked a hundred yards, again leaving clear prints. Luckily, I came to a stream. I stepped into the water and moved downstream several meters, then got out and moved farther downhill before turning north.

The only thing I knew in that direction was the interstate highway and I didn't have a clue how far away it was. The town of Oakland was to the south, but I was relying on them thinking I'd try to make my way there. It wouldn't work for long, but hopefully just long enough for me to get to a road or even better a farm from which I could call for help.

I could hear the rushing sound of water to my right. The area was laced with streams, but from the sound, I guessed it to be the Youghiogheny, which, according to the material Heather provided, is the main river in the area. I decided to move closer, to be able to use it as a guide to keep me heading in the right direction.

It turned out that I was only fifty yards from the river. The banks were steep, and the water was fast. Perfect for white water rafting, but deadly as hell if you accidentally fell in.

For an hour, I trudged along, and then I saw a rope suspension bridge at a point where the river cut through a hill, and my spirits lifted. I could cross the bridge and reverse course. It was getting late in the day, but I figured that I could cover a lot of ground before it got dark enough to be dangerous, and then I'd find a place to hole up until dawn. I kept my fingers crossed that they wouldn't have night vision goggles.

Once I'd settled into a steady pace, I had time to ponder my situation. It wasn't good.

I hadn't eaten since breakfast, and it was now 1:45 in the afternoon, although it looked later in the gloom of the trees. I was in unknown terrain, being pursued by armed men, and I had no food or water. I also had no weapons to speak of. A K-Bar is fine for close-in fighting, but against even a handgun, it's pretty puny unless the guy with the gun's facing the other way. Oh, and to cap it all off, I'd allowed someone to siphon gas from my means of transportation—the rental company was going to love hearing that one—and had been forced to leave a quarter million dollars of a client's money hidden in the woods. I didn't think it could possibly get any worse.

Of course, it did.

Chapter
Twenty

I made the dumbest, rookie mistake. I failed to pay enough attention to my surroundings, something I hadn't done since my first patrol as a young private when I walked over a ledge and landed on my face in a sewer ditch.

I'd been so lulled by the peaceful sounds of birds and the whisper of a breeze against the back of my neck I wandered into a clearing without first checking to see if the way was clear.

It wasn't. I didn't even notice at first that I

was in a clearing. The first thing that caught my attention was the sound of a voice off to my right, yelling in a language that I did not at first understand. When a geyser of dirt exploded about three feet in front of me, followed almost immediately by the popping sound of a large caliber handgun, my mind snapped back to the here and now real ricky-tick.

My brain went into overdrive. I recognized the language—Russian—even if I didn't understand what was being said. I also knew with certainty that I'd just been shot at. Fortunately for me, the shooter was as surprised as I was, and handguns are notoriously inaccurate unless you have the barrel pressed against the target, so in his haste, he'd over compensated. I didn't hesitate. I spun to my left and started to dive for cover in the little valley between the flat ground I was on and the hill.

Even a blind squirrel gets a nut now and then. Despite the inaccuracy of handguns, and because fate was giving me the middle finger for my stupidity, the shooter got lucky. Just as I was almost prone, I heard another 'pop' and almost simultaneously felt a sting in my left leg, in the meaty part of my thigh. By the time I was eating dirt and crawling for all I was worth toward a big tree, the stinging had become a burning sensation. It felt like someone had jabbed a hot poker into my leg.

I made it to the tree, rolled behind it, and

sat up, bracing my back against the rough trunk.

I heard a man's voice yell, "Cerzhant antisovetezm necobmectemi, mi obnaryoozhiv."

"Did you get him?" I heard the voice of the big man ask.

"Da, Sergeant Kolchak," the man replied. "I think I hit him in the leg."

I peeked around the tree, keeping as low a profile as possible. The big guy, Sergeant Kolchak, probably a former member of the Soviet *Spetznas*, now freelancing, stood there holding an AK-47. Next to him, a smaller man held a black handgun at his side. I'd been lucky, which is nice when you screw up. It could have been Kolchak with the AK who spotted me first. Unlike handguns, the assault rifle, in the hands of a trained marksman, would have been able to put several holes in my carcass before I was even fully aware of being shot at.

"Can you see him?" Kolchak asked.

"*Nyet, oh pozhel—*"

"In English, you idiot. How many times must I tell you, while here, we speak only English?"

"*Da, na angliskom,* uh, sorry, in English. He went down into some kind of hole, I think."

"We have to get him. Viktor will be very unhappy if we let him get away."

"But, he is on the other side of the river."

"I can see that, you fool. We need to find where he crossed, and follow him. Viktor wants him dead, do you understand?"

"*Da*, uh, I mean yes, sergeant."

The man spun and ran toward the north. Kolchak looked my way for a long time, then shook his head and followed.

They hadn't seen me, and they were a long way from the suspension bridge, so I had time to assess my situation.

It wasn't good, not good at all.

My pant leg was bloody, front and back. There was a slightly larger than a nickel sized hole in the front, and a smaller one in back. I stuck a finger in the front hole and ripped the fabric to get a look, and what I saw wasn't pretty. The hole in the front of my thigh was a tad smaller than a nickel. When I twisted my leg, and it hurt like the dickens when I did, I saw a much smaller hole in the back. Blood was oozing from both holes, which were on the outside of the thigh, the only good thing about the whole mess. The oozing blood meant the slug, probably a 9mm by the size of the entry wound, hadn't hit the femoral artery. Clip a hole in that, and you bleed out in minutes if a medic doesn't get to you. The other good thing was it didn't feel like the leg bones had been hit. That, too, would have been pretty bad. You can walk on a broken bone. It hurts pretty bad, but it can be done. But, if a bullet has chipped it, you can have bone fragments floating around, and the movement can cause pretty massive damage—damage of the unrepairable variety. And, I was wondering who the hell Viktor was.

The first thing I had to do was stop the bleeding. It takes longer, but a person with an untreated oozing wound can bleed to death if it's not treated.

I didn't have a first aid kit, but I remembered something my old Texas grandmother had taught me as a child. A paste of mud, with leaves as bandages, as nasty as it sounds, can plug a wound up until the blood clots. I'd worry about possible infection later. Using my K-Bar, I dug down until I found moist dirt, and daubed it over both holes. I then pressed some leaves over both, and tore off strips from my already ruined pant leg to tie them in place.

I needed to rest, but time wasn't on my side. It would take them an hour or less to find the bridge, and then another hour to get to where I was. I had to make good use of that time, and as much as I wanted to just lie back against that tree and go to sleep, I knew I had to move.

Hauling myself up took some effort, but I was finally able to stand upright without bracing myself against the tree. It hurt when I put pressure on the left leg, but I reminded myself that I'd endured worse. Once, when I was about ten, I'd fallen from a tree on my grandmother's farm. Fortunately, a fence was strung to the tree, so it broke my fall, and probably kept me from breaking my neck. Unfortunately, that fence was barbed wire, and it snagged my right leg, gashing my calf open. After I realized that screaming wouldn't help because I was too far from our house, I hoisted myself off, slapped mud in the gash, and walked the quarter mile to my grandmother's house, where she patched it up by cleaning it out, closing the flap of skin and slapping a piece of raw meat over it, which she bound to my leg with a piece of one of her white sheets. My parents had been livid that she hadn't taken me to a doctor for proper treatment, but it healed okay. It left a nice cigar-shaped scar that gave me bragging rights all the way through high school, but no other after effects. Now, I'd have two puckered scars on my upper thigh. I was a properly scarred veteran of the wars.

I made it up the side of the depression, and across a short ledge where I began to climb in earnest. After an hour of walking, the pain had subsided to just a dull, burning ache. Not unbearable, just annoying.

Oh, and I was pissed, too. And, it was the anger that kept me going.

Chapter
Twenty-One

By the time I I'd made it halfway to the top of the hill, the sun was already sinking low behind me in the west, and even though by my watch I'd only been climbing an hour, it felt like days. I was drenched with sweat, and the burning ache in my thigh had now spread to encompass my entire leg. It might have been a mistake to stop, but my lungs needed for my body to quit putting ridiculous demands upon them, at least for a few minutes. I found a tree with a nice thick trunk, put my back against it and slid down until my legs were splayed out in front of me.

I wanted so much to just stay there. A few minutes' rest would have felt *so* good. That's what the lazy part of my brain was telling me, like a little imp dressed in red on my shoulder. But, the biggest part of my brain was a snarling little imp dressed in camouflaged battle fatigues, and he was saying 'to hell with sleep. You can sleep after you get these goons off your trail.'

And, dammit, that's just what I intended to do. All those hours humping jungle and dessert, chasing narco-terrorists or just your plain old garden variety kill-innocents-to-send-a-message terrorists had taught me a few tricks I hoped my *Spetznas* friends might not be aware of.

I would have loved to be able to use a *punji* pit on them, but there just wasn't enough time to construct a proper one. Popular with the Viet Cong during our long war against them and the North Vietnamese, these trenches or holes lined with sharpened bamboo stakes called *punji* sticks were the cause of many an American GI getting a one-way ticket home. They sometimes dipped the sharpened end of the stakes in shit so they would cause infection. Nasty little buggers, but they were damned effective.

While a ditch filled with shit-dipped *punji*

stakes was off the menu, there were a few other little surprises that I could construct hastily.

The first trap I laid was a whip trap, one that the VC used to good advantage early in the war against American GIs on jungle patrol. It took me a while to find a suitable sapling close enough to the trail I'd been on, but after ten minutes of walking I saw the perfect one. About eight feet high and an inch thick at the base, it grew about a foot off the trail.

First, I cut off a two-foot length of branch and sharpened the end. I then bent the sapling down parallel to the trail and pulled it back until it was perpendicular. I cut a notch in the length of branch near the blunt end and hooked over the sapling and then pushed it into the ground to hold the sapling in place. I then had to find a way to weaponized it and trigger it. For weapons, I selected three straight twigs about a quarter inch in diameter and a foot long. After sharpening the ends, I found some vines back in the woods and affixed them about six inches apart with the first one three feet from the top of the sapling. Using a ten foot length of the same vine, I attached one end to the hook piece and threaded it around and across the trail on the side from which they would be following me, and about a quarter inch above the ground. I cut another twig and secured the end of the vine, tightening it.

Once I was satisfied it would pull the hook piece away when it was bumped even slightly, I covered it with leaves and twigs and stepped back to view my handiwork. Anyone coming up the trail behind me, unless he was paying close attention to the ground under his feet, wouldn't be aware of the vine until he felt the first resistance against his toe, by which time it would be too late. That pressure would pull the hook piece free, allowing the sapling to whip around in an effort to return to its upright position. I figured it would swing almost horizontally across the trail about crotch high before returning to the upright, and at least one, if not two, of the sharpened stakes would strike flesh. In that part of the body they wouldn't have to penetrate too deeply to take any pursuers mind off me and onto a precious part of his anatomy. If they were walking single file, it would only reduce the pursuing force by one, but it would cause those remaining to slow their chase as they looked for additional booby traps.

It wasn't much of an advantage, but it was better than nothing. I wouldn't have to go slow to avoid booby traps.

I was feeling pretty good with myself as I headed a hundred yards farther up the trail, looking for a place to set my next trap.

The place that presented itself was a natural. The trail pinched in by a tree to the right and a thick clump of bush to the right was less than three feet wide. There was no way to get off it without going back several feet, and the trail itself was covered with a thick layer of dead leaves. If I'd had time, and a shovel, I would've dug a good *pungi* pit, but, lacking that, I settled for the next best thing.

Using my K-Bar, I dug a square hole, six inches deep and eighteen inches on each side, in the center of the trail. I then installed two small branches on each side, two inches apart and starting four inches from the sides. I then found two branches that were about an inch in diameter with smaller branches near the ends. I trimmed and sharpened two or three of the small branches, all on one side, and lay one on each of the two-branch shelves I'd created, with the sharpened twigs pointing up. I places them end-to-end, meeting in the center of my pit. Once they were adjusted to my satisfaction, I created a lattice work of twigs and placed it over the pit and then covered that with leaves and dirt, brushing things around until the pit blended into the surrounding area.

I would have preferred having flat boards with nails, but you work with what you have. This particular variation on a VC booby trap wasn't fatal, but it played hell with your ability to maneuver. When someone stepped on it, the two studded pieces sank in the middle, coming up like a fan or clapper, and the pointed ends penetrated an ankle or lower leg. It wouldn't necessarily kill you, but with holes in your ankle or leg, you don't feel much like humping the boonies any more. If my swing trap got 'em, and I was pretty sure it would, and then they were so intent on looking for tripwires, someone stepped into this one and got an ankle punctured, the chase would really slow down.

A third successful booby trap would probably be out of the question, but I'd have given myself a huge edge with just these two.

Things were looking up.

Chapter
Twenty-Two

While I would like to have stuck around and seen the results of my handiwork, the shadows of late afternoon were lengthening into evening, and I knew I had to extend the gap between my pursuers as much as possible before it became too dark to navigate the mountain.

I stayed on the trail for another hundred yards, by which time the shadows of the trees west of the trail had crept completely across, shrouding it in murkiness. The temperature had dropped, sucking tendrils of mist from the soil and dead vegetation of the forest floor. I needed to find a place to spend the night.

I swung left and began climbing again, looking for a place that would provide shelter while allowing me to keep watch on the trail. A tall order with the darkness coming on like a tsunami. Visual surveillance wouldn't be possible, but above the trail I should be able to hear anything approaching from any direction.

About twenty yards above the trail, I found a little ridge jutting out from the base of a large tree; a flat area of about three square feet, covered in dead leaves, open on two sides, one of them being the downhill side. It wasn't ideal, but it was getting darker and there was no time to look for a better place.

I scooped up dry leaves and pine straw from the surrounding area and dumped it onto the ledge. Then, I sat with my back against the bole of the tree and my injured leg stuck straight out in front.

As it does in the area where I live, far from the ever present lights of the city and suburbs, darkness on the mountain, when it came was deep and as heavy as a down comforter, and equally soothing. Far from being afraid of the dark, I welcomed it. Sitting there, my back against the rough bark of a tree, I could meditate fully, the call of night birds and insects soothing rather than distracting, and allow my senses to operate at full capacity. We humans tend to rely too much on the sense of sight, one that evolution has not developed in humans to the degree it has in an animal like an eagle. It is, in fact, one of the weakest of our senses. One that is more valuable, better developed than vision, and that we often ignore, is hearing. When the ears are not distracted, they pick up the subtle sounds that we often miss. The whisper of a soft wind across leaves, the chitter of insects crawling through the grass; they make their way into our consciousness when we're in 'hearing' mode, rather than when we try to 'listen' for them.

My senses of smell and touch also kicked in. I could smell the different odor of the leaves after the evening condensation settled on them, and I could feel the soft caress of the evening air as convection currents wafted up from the cooling earth.

At some point, without even being aware of it, I fell asleep. I know this, because the feel of moisture, the bite of a morning chill, and the ache in my thigh all hit me at once and my eyes snapped open to a view of the sky which was the color of steam-fogged aluminum. My throat was dry and raspy, and my stomach was making gurgling sounds. My back felt stiff and I had a slight pain in my neck.

And, I was royally pissed off. I'd been upset all along, and that's what had kept me going. But now, the anger I felt was not the kind that keeps you up and moving, it was the kind that made you want to smash things.

This Kolchak and his Russian friends had caused me to miss lunch and supper, and my stomach was aching from hunger. I'd run through the forest, unable to take time to find a source of fresh water, and was feeling weak from dehydration. And, I had holes in my leg where they'd shot me.

Dammit, I was—am—Al Pennyback. I don't run from the bad guys, I chase the bad guys. I'm not the violent, aggressive type, but I don't take shit from anyone either, and these guys had dumped a lot of crap on my head in less than twenty-four hours.

Well, I thought as I slowly flexed my left leg to ease the stiffness and pain, and then pushed myself to a standing position, Al Pennyback was through running.

It was payback time.

The hunters were just about to become the hunted.

Chapter
Twenty-Three

I checked my watch. It was 5:05. The sun wouldn't be up for an hour, but Kolchak and his goons were probably already up, making their way slowly and cautiously—I hoped—on the trail I'd made no effort to conceal.

Time for me to move.

I moved slowly, as much from the pain in my leg as from caution, back down toward my original trail. About ten feet above it, and from a position from which I could see at least fifty feet in both directions, I stopped. Looking down, I saw no other markings than my own on the trail, but noticed that my own trail did end at the point where I began my ascent up the hill. No way would my pursuers miss that. I worked my way parallel to my back trail until I was a hundred feet away from that point, then settled back to wait. It wasn't as good a vantage point as the other, I could only see ten or so feet back toward my night resting place, and fifteen in the other direction, but it would allow me to get behind them before they realized that I'd left the trail.

Once I was satisfied that I was adequately concealed, I settled in to do what soldiers have done before battle for millennia, I waited.

The secret to surviving the waiting is learning to keep your mind focused on your mission without becoming obsessed with it.

My attention moved from the back trail, to which I paid the most attention, to the trail ahead. I was pretty sure the Russians would be following my trail, but I couldn't assume they hadn't passed me by either, and, having discovered they'd passed me, come back from the trail ahead.

After two hours of waiting, during which time, the sun had risen quite high and the shadows had shortened, my initial assumption was proven correct.

I recognized the first man to come around the bend in the trail; he was the galoot who'd plugged me with a lucky shot. He held a nasty looking black side arm at his right side that was too far away for me to recognize. He was making his way up the trail slowly, looking intently at the ground in front before moving his feet forward, and checking the side of the trail up to eye level. This was confirmation that my booby traps had been successful. At the rate he was moving, even with my bum leg, I could move through the bush at a much faster rate of speed, and he was so intent on the trail, he never even looked my way.

Twenty feet behind him, the big guy, Kolchak, cradling an AK-47 across his chest, moved just as slowly, and copied the lead man's actions in checking the trail.

I was just about to move to get behind them, when the third man appeared. He, too, carried a sidearm, held loosely against his right thigh. He was thirty feet behind Kolchak and walked with a limp, favoring his right leg. His right pants leg had a large dark spot on the outside, just above the top of his boot. He'd stepped on my second trap. I'd hoped it would pierce his boot and hit near his ankle, which would have made it almost impossible to walk, but it had apparently stabbed his calf well above the ankle. He could walk, but the way he moved, he was in a lot of pain, and was having trouble keeping up with the other two. He was also intently studying the terrain at his feet, which added to the difficulty in maintaining a consistent distance between himself and Kolchak. This gave me an idea.

To the right, the trail curved away from the river. This meant that when Kolchak went around the bend, there would be several seconds when the third man would be out of sight of the others.

When Kolchak passed my position, I began working my way down the hill, keeping to the bushes until I was in a thick stand of vegetation about two feet off the trail.

Just as I'd expected him to, the third man walked past without glancing in my direction, he was so intent on not stepping in another trap, I could probably have been standing in the open and he wouldn't have noticed me. When he was two paces past my position, I stepped out behind him. My injured left leg caused me to drag my foot, making a soft sound against the hard earth, alerting him to my presence, but not soon enough.

As he started his turn, opening his mouth to shout a warning to his comrades, I slapped my left hand tightly over his mouth and pinched his nostrils closed with my thumb and forefinger. At the same time, I slipped my thumb between his thumb and the butt of his sidearm and wrapped my last two fingers around his little finger, pulling back on it with all my strength. He released his grip on the weapon, and I pulled it away and tossed it into the brush. Then, I pressed my right forearm against his throat and pulled him against my chest, squeezing until I was certain I'd blocked his breathing.

He struggled and made incoherent mumbling noises against my sweaty palm, but was hampered in his movement by the combination of the pain in his right leg and the panic that's caused when suddenly you're unable to pull air into your lungs. My intent, though, was not just to deprive him of oxygen. Contrary to what you see in the movies, it can take up to five minutes of air deprivation for some to pass out, and a bit longer to choke someone to death, and I didn't have that much time. When I wrapped my right arm around his throat, I compressed his carotid to disrupt the blood flow to his brain. That causes unconsciousness in a few seconds. He struggled, grasping at my forearm, but was unable to force me to loosen my grip, and sure enough, after ten seconds, his body went limp.

I loosened my hold on his neck and relaxed my finger and thumb to allow him to breath. Frankly, considering what he and his friends had intended to do to me, I wasn't too concerned that I might have deprived him of air and blood long enough to cause permanent brain damage. If this had been combat, I would have kept his air cut off until he was dead, but I'm not into casual killing. He'd be out of action for several minutes, and be groggy as hell when he came around. That would give me time to do what I needed to do. I dragged him off the trail and dumped his unconscious form under some bushes. I then killed a few more seconds retrieving his sidearm, a Glock 17, 9mm. He also had an old U.S. Army canteen hooked to his belt, which I relieved him of. It was half full and the water was warm, but after nearly a full day without water, I didn't care. I took a long drink, swishing some around in my mouth to relieve the dryness, and held it in my throat as well. Warm or not, it tasted better than the finest wine.

Using the clips on the canteen, I hooked it to my belt, and shoved the Glock into my belt at the small of my back, and melted into the bush upslope.

It didn't take me as long as I thought it would have to make my way in front of Kolchak and my shooter. The two of them continued to creep along the trail looking out for any more booby traps. Kolchak seemed totally unaware that his third man was no longer behind him.

As I walked, I mulled plans over in my mind. I needed to change the odds in my favor, and even with the Glock my chances against two of them, one armed with an AK, weren't good. Kolchak was the more dangerous of the two, but he was also in charge. That meant that he had answers to the many questions running through my mind.

By default, that meant that the point man was expendable. Now, I only had to figure a way to get him out of the way so I could come up with a way to take Kolchak down.

Easier said than done. The trail going forward had as many bends as it did behind them, but both men were uninjured and even they moved at a slow pace, they kept a pretty decent interval, which didn't give me as much time as I'd had with the injured third man.

I would have to catch the point man at a point when he was out of Kolchak's sight and take him down in a matter of seconds. And, I would have to do it silently to avoid alerting Kolchak.

If I could've gotten in close enough to apply the same choke hold I'd used on his comrade that would have been great. But, uninjured, he was more alert, and I couldn't be sure I'd have enough time before Kolchak came in sight. Shooting him, even if I'd been so inclined, was out of the question, because the sound of the shot would alert Kolchak.

I was running options through my mind at a rapid pace, and discarding them as impractical just as quickly. My left foot, still unwieldy, bumped against a fallen tree branch. I looked down as I lifted my foot to step over the branch, and the perfect plan popped into my mind.

Sometimes, simple is best. In this case, simple involved brute force. It wasn't an elegant plan, but I was confident it would work.

I picked the branch up. It was about four feet long and two inches in diameter. It felt like it weighed about five pounds, and it hadn't been on the ground long enough to have deteriorated much. In other words, it made a nice sap, club, bat; whatever you want to call it.

When the point man made the next right turn in the trail, I let him take four steps forward and stepped out of the bush behind him. Some sixth sense alerted him to my presence, but he didn't even get to turn as far as his friend did before I brought the branch around in a left hand swing like I'd used when batting off hand in high school baseball and was going for the outfield fence. The wood made a 'whack' sound like a bat makes when it makes contact with a fast ball. He made an 'oomph' sound as his eyes rolled back in their sockets and he slumped to the ground like one of those air-filled mannequins when you turn the air pump off. I breathed a sigh of relief. I'd thought I might have to hit him more than once to take him down. After tossing the branch off the trail, I grabbed his unconscious form by the shoulders and pulled him up the slope and laid him under some bushes. I didn't know how long he'd be out, but a goose egg-sized lump had already formed on the back of his skull, and he'd have one hell of a headache whenever he did wake up.

I then went back to near the edge of the trail and crouched in the bush, just as Kolchak came around the bend in the trail.

A few steps in, he stopped, peering ahead. The trail turned about fifty feet in front of him, but he stared at it with a puzzled frown. Then, he looked around. His expression said that something was amiss, but with a hint of uncertainty. He moved forward slowly, dividing his attention between the ground and the sides of the trail. He walked past me, almost close enough to touch, and luckily was looking down to see where he was putting his feet, or he might have spotted me.

When he was three steps past me, I took the Glock from my belt and stepped out behind him. He froze, one foot still off the ground, and I could see the muscles in his shoulder stiffen.

Before he could turn, I stepped up and put the muzzle of the Glock against the small of his back.

"I can't miss up this close," I said. "And, if you make a sudden move, you're gonna get a 9mm slug in the spine. I don't need to tell you what that'll do to you. Now drop the AK, and kick it away."

He hesitated. I jabbed him hard enough to cause pain. Wisely, he dropped the rifle and gave it a kick that sent it spinning five feet away.

"You are a resourceful man," he said through clenched teeth. "Your booby traps were excellent. I'm not sure Mikhail survived the one that stabbed him in the cock, but even if he does, he will never be a father now. I imagine my other two men are dead?"

I felt no compassion for this Mikhail, but saw no reason to let him know that his other two goons were just sleeping in the bushes.

"Right now, you should just be glad that you're alive."

"So, what will you do? Tie me up, or kill me, and make your escape?"

"None of the above," I said. He twisted his head around and shot a puzzle look at me. "You and I are going for a little walk, and then a ride. I want to talk to your boss."

Chapter
Twenty-Four

I kept Kolchak in front of me as we backtracked. The two men I'd 'taken care of' were still out for the count when we passed where I'd stashed them just off the trail. I still left him in the dark as to whether or not they were still alive, but smiled at the thought that they'd eventually wake up and discover that they had a long walk home ahead of them.

When we arrived at the spot where I'd set the first booby trap, it turned out that Kolchak had guessed right. The trap had worked even better than I'd anticipated, impaling the man who'd been on point in the groin and upper thigh. He'd been left to fend for himself. Unfortunately, one of the stakes must have nicked his femoral artery. He'd bled out sitting there beside the trail. The front of his pants from the crotch down to the knee was a sticky, black mess where the blood that had seeped from his body was starting to congeal. He sat with his back against a small tree; his sightless eyes the target of flies that had been attracted to the blood.

Kolchak kept walking, his eyes averted from the scene.

"Don't you want to stop and at least bury him?" I asked.

"It does not matter to him now whether or not he is buried," he said simply, and kept walking.

Whoever was paying the freight must have been paying well. I couldn't see anyone sane working with this cold-blooded son of a bitch, but I kept my thoughts to myself and kept the business end of the AK pointed at his back. When we arrived at my rented 4-Runner I had him stop.

"Why are we stopping here?" he asked. "There is no fuel in this vehicle."

"We're not taking the car. I'll pick it up

later. But, I do have a parcel to retrieve."

I smiled at his look of confusion.

"You mean the money?" he asked. "It was not in the vehicle, and I assumed you pitched out somewhere along the road."

"Well, bucko, you assumed wrong." I motioned with the AK and got him moving toward the bushes in which I'd secreted the case of cash.

When I pushed him into the undergrowth and used the barrel to push aside the bush concealing the case, his confusion transformed into a look of . . . well, I'd have to say respect.

"So, it was here all along. You continue to surprise me."

"I have another surprise for you," I said. "You're hauling that out of here to your truck, and I have to warn you, it's pretty damn heavy."

He didn't react, didn't even blink. He just hefted the case and slung it across his left shoulder. I motioned him toward the 4-Runner and kept him covered with the AK while I retrieved my backpack and two bottles of warm-to-the-touch water. I put the backpack on my left shoulder and one of the bottles of water in my pocket. I tossed him the other.

"Just hours ago, my men and I were trying to kill you," he said. "Before the day is over, I might again. Yet, you are kind enough to give me water. You Americans are strange people."

"You speak pretty good English for a Russian," I said. "You sound more like a former KGB operative than Spetznas." That got a slight reaction, a momentary widening of the eyes, which he quickly got under control. "Anyway, I'm not being generous. I need you strong to hump that money to your pickup. Can't have you fainting from dehydration on me now can I?"

He laughed. "Very practical. I am thinking you, too, are a soldier?"

"I was, but I've been out of the army for a long time."

"How do you Americans say it . . . like riding the bicycle, you never forget? I knew when we encountered the first trap that you were more than just a messenger."

There was nothing I could say to that. He was observant. But then, he'd been trained to be observant, just as I had. So, I said nothing.

Roughly thirty minutes later, we reached the road. His pickup was parked with the right side wheels well off the road.

"Put the money in the back," I said, taking my backpack off and tossing it over the tailgate. "Then, get in behind the wheel."

I kept him covered until he was seated behind the wheel and belted in. I then got into the passenger side and put the AK on my lap with the muzzle just inches from his side and my finger a fraction of an inch away from the trigger.

"Please be careful with that," he said. "This is a bumpy road. I would hate to have you shoot me by accident."

I hoped to hell it wouldn't come to me having to shoot him. I hadn't shot a man in years, the last time was a rogue FBI agent who was about to put a bullet into me.

"Don't worry, if I shoot you, it won't be an accident. Now, drive, and take it nice and slow."

He did, never exceeding thirty miles an hour, and more often than not, going between fifteen and twenty, glancing over at me every few minutes and then down at the assault rifle. I kept my eye on him.

When I estimated we were about half a mile from the sentry post, I ordered him to pull over and stop.

"Why are we stopping here?" He looked like he wanted to ignore my instructions, but did it anyway.

"I need answers to a few questions before I meet your boss."

He shrugged and draped his hands on the steering wheel.

"I do not know much, but ask what you will," he said.

"Let's start with this place. How did a bunch of Russians get hooked up with an American militia?"

"You mean these fat Americans who play at being soldiers? They are Viktor's customers, so when he needed a place to stay, they were happy to provide this place for us."

"Customers? I would never have thought of a bunch of right-wing types as art connoisseurs."

"They have no interest in art," he said. "They buy weapons. Art is not the only commodity that Viktor deals in. He sells many weapons, and America is second only to the Middle East in the number of customers."

"You keep referring to Viktor. I assume that's Wesley Hendriks?"

"*Da*, yes, Hendriks is the name he uses with his American customers. His real name is Viktor Ivanov."

This was an interesting tidbit that I planned to pass along to my buddy, Buster Mayweather, to share with his federal cop friends. Buster's a DC Metro Police detective, and like most local cops, needs all the leverage he can get when dealing with the feds. Local militia groups buying arms from the Russian mob just might be the kind of information that would impress the suits.

"Is he also former *Spetznas* like you and your friends?"

He laughed. "Viktor in the military . . . as you Americans say, no way. Like his father before him, Viktor was in the KGB. When the Soviet Union fell apart, like so many of us, he found the new Russian Federation a difficult place to live, so he entered the . . . private sector."

"So, whatever is in demand, to the highest bidder?"

"He is now very rich man." He shrugged. "He pays very well. I do not understand something. He sent us to kill you. Why are you not going in the opposite direction to get away from here?"

"Let me ask you a question . . . does he have this painting he tried to sell to my client?"

"Yes, he has it."

"Then, there are two reasons I'm going to see him. First, I was hired to do a job, so I intend to complete it. Secondly, I don't particularly like it when someone tries to kill me. I wish to make that point very clear to him."

His eyebrows arched upwards. "Does this mean that you also have unfinished business with me?"

"Nothing personal, Kolchak," I said. "But, you are merely a tool. My beef's with the craftsman, and that's Ivanov. If you come after me again, though, then I *will* take it personally."

He looked at me for a long time, several seconds, and then his thin lips curved upwards.

"*Da*, you are soldier. We understand each other. I think I would not want to be Viktor right now. So, are you ready to go and see him?"

"What time do the militia men eat supper?"

"They eat between 5:30 and 6:30. Ah, I understand, at that time, only the two guards near the entrance to the compound are alert. If I am driving, though, they will not challenge us."

"I'm not worried about that," I said. "I just don't want anyone interfering with my meeting with Ivanov."

"So, after you have had your . . . talk with him, and you have the painting, will you also keep the money?"

"No, Kolchak, my job was to exchange the money for the painting, and that's what I'll do, although, I'm not sure Mr. Ivanov will be in such good shape to appreciate his new-found wealth."

"Is not for you to worry. I am sure someone will find use for so much money." He smiled a vulpine, predatory smile that sent chills up my spine. "Now, we wait. Oh, and you can call me Ivan, *tovarich.*"

Chapter
Twenty-Five

At 5:35, I had him fire up the engine and start driving toward the militia compound.

As he'd said, we blew past the sentries without a challenge. They just waved. There was no sign of the militia around the Quonset huts, so I assumed everyone was at evening chow. I had Kolchak drive across the grass and park in front of the cabin. I kept the AK on him as I exited, and then, holding it with the muzzle pointing down, but in a way that I could easily bring it back up, I motioned for him to get out of the pickup.

He walked toward the back of the pickup, reaching for the case.

"Leave the money," I said. "I'll get it when your boss has produced the painting."

He frowned at me. "It will be easier to convince him to do that if he can see the money."

That was a good point. "Okay, bring it along." I pointed the AK toward the cabin door. "You go in first."

He pulled the case out and easily slung it across his left shoulder. I grabbed my backpack, and followed behind him as he opened the door and entered.

His bulk and the case initially blocked my view of Hendriks/Ivanov, but I could hear the scraping as the chair behind the desk moved.

"You got him, and the money—" Ivanov's eyes went round like saucers when I stepped from behind Kolchak and pointed the AK at him.

"No, the other way around," I said. "I got him. Now, I'm here to get the painting you promised my client."

His hands, which had been on the desk as if he was about to balance with them to stand, started moving slowly back toward his body, and his eyes darted downward. I pointed the AK at his chest.

"Uh-uh, keep those hands where I can see them," I said.

His eyes narrowed, and his lips quivered as he frowned.

"I would do as he says," Kolchak said. "He took out three of my men, and was able to sneak up on me with the weapons he took from them."

Even from across the room, I could see Ivanov assessing the odds, and trying to decide whether he could get to the weapon I was pretty sure he had in the desk drawer, and the shadow that crossed his face as he realized that I could spray him with a storm of slugs before he ever got his hand around the grip.

"You know, it might be a good idea if you stood and came from behind that desk," I said. "I wouldn't want you tempted to try and get a weapon. It's hard to do business with a dead man."

Ivanov had the look of someone who was accustomed to giving orders and having others do his dirty work. From the murderous look he gave me, he clearly didn't like *taking* orders. But, he was also no fool. He kept his hands in sight as he stood and walked to the side of the desk.

"And, just what business do you wish to do?"

"You offered to sell my client a painting." I pointed to the case slung from Kolchak's shoulder. "The amount you requested, seven hundred and fifty thousand dollars, is inside that case. You get me the painting, and it's yours."

"What will you do if I refuse?"

"You don't want to know. Now, how about that painting?"

What I really wanted to do was to rearrange the features on his face. I'd led Kolchak to believe that I might be seeking revenge for him sending men to kill me. I wasn't sure if I wanted to do that now or not.

"I am afraid we have a small problem," he said. "You see, I never intended to convey that painting to . . . Mr. Chester Boulware."

Now it was my turn to stand there with my mouth agape. Kolchak chuckled.

"At any rate," Ivanov went on. "His name is not even Chester Boulware."

"I knew that," I said. It sounded lame as soon as the words were out of my mouth, and I'm not even sure why I said it, but it did cause a look of surprise to flicker on his face.

"You know that he is an imposter, and you still agree to work for him?"

"The pay's good." I shrugged.

"Ah ha," he said. "So, you know who he is not, but you do not know who he *is*."

My expression answered his question.

"So, you do not know. Well, my American friend, I will tell you who he really is. His true name is Kurt Richter."

"How do you know this?" I asked.

"Because, I have been looking for him for more than forty years. I tracked him from Magdeburg to England to America. Before now, he has always been one step ahead of me. I lost his trail twenty years ago, but his obsession with art led me to him here."

"Why are you so interested in this Kurt Richter?"

He laughed, but there was no mirth in it. "I see no harm in telling you, because you will not leave this place alive to—"

"Whoa, friend," I interrupted. "I'm the one with the gun. Who's gonna stop me from leaving?"

"My friend, Mr. Shelton and his toy soldiers might look ineffective, and in truth, against a real army they would be useless. But, I assure you they are more than capable of dealing with one man." He looked down at my bloodstained trouser leg. "And, an injured one at that. I know what you're thinking; you can kill Ivan and me, but if you do that, they will hear the shots and be upon you immediately."

I kept my mouth shut. I had no intention of shooting and alerting the militia goons.

"I'll take my chances," I said. "Won't do you much good if you're dead though, now will it? Now, mind telling me why you're so keen on getting to Boulware, I mean, Richter?"

"Oh, I plan to kill him. Kurt Richter is the only son of Capitan Werner Richter, a member of Hitler's SS. Richter was the commander of the SS unit near Magdeburg during the Great Patriotic War. His job was to secure the salt mine in which the Nazis kept stored the art work they stole from all over Europe. When the Soviet Army took over the area after the Americans had liberated it, my father, Vladimir Ivanov, and his unit found the mine, which the Americans had overlooked. The Americans had also failed to capture Richter and some of his men. My father managed to get several of the pieces from the mine and hide them in the nearby forest. He got a few of the smaller works back to the Soviet Union, but about a year after the end of the war, just as he was getting ready to ship the remainder back, Richter discovered his hiding place. He killed my father and stole the paintings."

"Okay, so this Richter character killed your father, why don't you go after him?"

"Unfortunately, Werner Richter died twenty years ago, when I lost his son's trail. He has the other paintings that were taken from that mine. I will kill him and take them back. My father's ghost will be appeased."

Chapter
Twenty-Six

Ivanov presented me with quite a dilemma. My client, though, presented me with an even greater one.

Solving Ivanov's was my first priority. I had no desire to kill him or Kolchak, but I couldn't allow them to alert the militia either. I had to take them out of action long enough to make my getaway. Thankfully, I had, in the bottom of my backpack, the means to do it, and quietly.

I eased the backpack off my shoulder and dropped it on the floor.

"Get that chair from behind the desk," I told Kolchak. "And, move it around in front of it."

He looked confused, but dropped the canvas bag and complied. I then motioned for Ivanov to sit in the chair. When Ivanov was seated, with an angry look on his face, and Kolchak was standing beside him, still looking puzzled, I knelt—keeping the AK on them—and felt around in my backpack until I found the coil of rope. I pulled it out and began uncoiling it. When I had about ten feet uncoiled, I took out my K-Bar and whacked off three sections, each about three feet long.

"Tie his hands behind the back of the chair, and his ankles to the front," I said, kicking the lengths of rope toward Kolchak. "And, make the knots good and tight."

When he was done, I motioned him aside and checked his work. Kolchak didn't care much for his boss. The rope was so tight Ivanov's fingertips were turning pale. Good, I thought, the SOB would suffer a little. I decided to add to that suffering.

"Take his shoes and socks off," I said.

While he knelt to comply with my order, I quickly cut three more lengths of rope.

Kolchak had to brace himself against Ivanov's knees and tilt the chair back in order to remove the leather combat boots, which fortunately had Velcro snaps rather than laces. When he pulled off the first black sock, he made a face. Seconds later I understood why. Ivanov had a major foot odor problem, the kind even Odor Eaters can't cure. A smell like the kind that comes from the bottom of a laundry hamper full of moist, dirty clothes, hit my nose like a jab from Mike Tyson. I held my breath as Kolchak, holding them gingerly between the tip of his index finger and thumb, thrust the socks at me.

"What do you plan to do with these?" he asked.

"You've heard of putting your foot in your mouth? Well, I plan to use one of these to gag your boss." I held them as far away from my face as possible, copying his technique of pinching them between the tips of my finger and thumb.

"What do you plan to do with the other?" The sickly expression on his face said that he had a suspicion. I nodded at him. "Please, I would rather you cut the sleeve off my shirt."

Ivanov looked from him to me with a murderous glare on his face.

"You cannot do this," he said.

I could, I would, and I did. Or, rather, I had Kolchak do it. As he stuffed the sock into his boss's mouth, Ivanov looked like he wanted to puke, which wouldn't have been smart, since he was likely to choke to death. Kolchak didn't seem bothered by the prospect. I had him tear the right sleeve off Ivanov's jacket and use it to hold the gag in place. Tears were rolling freely from Ivanov's eyes, whether from his efforts to breathe through his nose, anger, or frustration, I wasn't sure—and didn't much care.

Once Ivanov was firmly trussed up and gagged, I turned to Kolchak.

"Now, your turn," I said. "Sit down beside the desk and put your feet underneath it."

He had to twist his feet to the side, and his thick calves caused his shins to brush against the bottom of the desk, but he was finally sitting in such a way that he couldn't move quickly. I stepped behind him and securely tied his arms behind his back, looping the thin rope over his thumbs so that he wouldn't be able to quickly work his way out of the bindings. Next, I spread his legs and tied one to each of the desk legs. It was an uncomfortable position for him to be in, but it was also one that wouldn't be easy for him to get at the ropes. The two of them would, I hoped, be immobile long enough for me to make my getaway.

"You do not intend to use Viktor's sock to gag me, I hope," he said.

It was tempting. After all, he'd tried to kill me. But, since his capture, he'd been on pretty good behavior, and he was just a hired hand.

I cut his left sleeve off and then cut it into strips.

"Would you prefer this?"

He nodded vigorously. Ivanov made strangling sounds behind his gag. I crumpled up one of the strips and shoved it into Kolchak's mouth, and then wrapped the other strip around his head to hold it in place.

I stepped back to admire my handiwork. Ivanov continued to glare up at me. Kolchak's expression was unreadable. He shrugged when I fished the pickup keys from his pocket, and I could have sworn his lips turned up in a smile.

I picked up the money case and slung it over my left shoulder, and then picked up my backpack, holding it in my left hand, leaving my right free for the AK. After opening the door a tiny crack to see if anyone was in the immediate vicinity, and seeing or hearing nothing, I pulled it open the rest of the way and stepped outside.

Charles Ray

Chapter
Twenty-Seven

I'd stowed the money and was just about to toss my backpack into the back of the pickup when I heard the steps behind me.

I turned to find a skinny guy in cammies with an AR-15 on his shoulder coming around the corner of the cabin. When he saw me, his little piggy eyes went wide and he started to yank the rifle off his shoulder.

"Where the fuck you think you're—"

I took a quick step forward and did the only thing I could think of doing to stop him from giving the alarm; I kicked him in the balls with my right foot, feeling the mushiness of his junk and then the hardness of whatever bones I'd smashed against. His words were cut off, and he made a sound like a mouse that was just speared by a hawk's talons. His eyes got bigger and full of tears, and he forgot all about the rifle he was reaching for, grabbing instead at his smashed gonads as he sank to his knees.

As he bent forward, making mewling sounds and cupping his balls, I raised the AK and smashed it against his forehead. His head rocked back and then he pitched forward. The mewling stopped.

I felt a little guilty not stopping to check and see if he was still breathing, but I really didn't want to chance someone else dropping by, so I jumped into the cab of the pickup, tossed the AK onto the passenger seat, inserted the key and fired the engine.

I shoved the gear into reverse, backed up to give myself turning room, then threw it into drive and pressed the gas pedal to the floor. The rear wheels spun up a cloud of brown dust before biting into the earth. The big truck jerked forward like a plane being catapulted off a carrier deck, slamming me back into the seat back. As the vehicle settled down, I swayed forward, my chest bumping the steering wheel. I realized that in my haste to get out of Dodge, I'd neglected to clip on the seatbelt. As dangerous as that is, though, I had no intention of taking a hand off the wheel long enough to remedy the situation.

As I approached the sentry posts, one of them foolishly stepped out onto the road and raised his hand. I didn't slow down, and he was too slow stepping out of the way. The pickup clipped him, not a full-blown smash, but enough to send him tumbling into the bush. In the rearview mirror I saw the other sentry start to raise his rifle, and then decide to help his comrade, and then the scene behind me disappeared in the rooster tail of dust I was creating.

He wouldn't be distracted long, though. It was a matter of minutes until he alerted his friends, and I'd have the Russians *and* the militia on my tail.

And, just before I reached the intersection with the big dirt road, they *were* on my tail. They signaled that fact by sending several rounds through the back window of the pickup, a fact I became aware of when I heard the *pop, snap,* of high velocity rounds penetrating the glass, and saw the little circles with spider web radials emanating from them in the right front window.

I hunched over the wheel, my head just

high enough to see over the hood and stay on the road. Their lousy marksmanship, the difficulty of hitting anything while shooting from a moving, bouncing vehicle, and the many turns in the road—and a huge bit of luck—kept them from hitting anything other than the truck, and even those hits, after the first lucky volley, were seldom, just an occasional *thunk* as a round struck the heavy metal body.

When it hits the fan and the bullets start flying, a strange thing happens to time. It seems to stand still and race forward at the same time. Some moments or events appear to move in slow motion, or not at all, like an insect suspended in amber, while others zip by, just blurs on the periphery of your vision.

That's what it felt like during that mad chase along a twisting, serpentine dirt road that was little more than tire tracks on the hard earth with a line of browned, dust-covered vegetation marking its midpoint. The road ahead of me, or what I could see of it over the edge of the dashboard, seemed to stretch on to infinity, and my journey over it unraveled agonizingly slow, while, the glimpses of the dust-cloud-covered road behind me were like a speeded-up movie film.

I hit the main dirt road, and almost shot across and into the trees lining it, but was able to whip the wheel to the right in time to keep the pickup more or less on the graded portion, although the left-side rear wheel did slide into the shallow ditch for a moment, before biting into the gritty clay and shooting me again forward. The dust cloud behind me became thicker, hiding my pursuers from my view, but at the same time, making it damn near impossible for them to see me, and as a consequence hit me with their wild shots. In addition, the possibility of other traffic on this more-traveled road probably inhibited them.

I tried to goose more speed from the truck, getting up to a hair-raising, spine-tingling 60 mph. Every bump in the road was magnified, sending my head into the metal overhead and jarring my teeth. I no longer heard the *ping* of bullets striking the pickup, but I couldn't be sure they were no longer shooting at me. The roar of the truck's engine drowned out all other sounds.

The mad chase seemed to be never ending, thus, when I saw the gray ribbon ahead that was the highway it caught me by surprise. I recovered just in time to make a jerky turn right, fishtailing into the oncoming lane for a few seconds, and finally getting myself lined up and in the proper lane.

I glanced in the interior rearview mirror. There wasn't much rear window left, but the highway behind me was clear. The militia must have given up when I made the highway. I eased off the gas and let my speed drop to 50 mph, keeping it there even after entering an area with a 35 mph limit.

There never seems to be a cop around when you need one. Which, actually, was probably for the best. I'd been hoping to get pulled over so I could explain why I was driving like a madman and get the cops into the hills, but as I entered Oakland, and dropped to the speed limit, I noticed the AK on the passenger seat and realized how fortunate I was not to have been pulled over by cop on the road. Sure, I had bullet holes in the windows, and no doubt bullet holes in the rear of the truck, but an assault rifle on the seat together with the bullet holes, to a nervous county cop, could look like a drug war or a drug deal gone bad. The color of my skin wouldn't help my case either. I let out a sigh of relief as I pulled into the parking lot near the county police building. The fates sometimes look out for people who make foolish decisions.

I pulled into an empty parking slot near the street, and before getting out of the truck, I put the AK on the floor so it wouldn't be spotted by some casual passerby. Then, I got out and limped to the building.

Chapter
Twenty-Eight

The bloody trouser leg and the limp got me immediate attention. A young uniformed cop rushed to my aid, helping me to a chair near the desk sergeant's station, while at the same time asking me what happened.

The next few minutes were a blur. I had two or three cops firing questions at me while an EMT cut away my trouser leg and began treating my wound. The darkening and puckered hole in my thigh *really* got their attention, and the questions started coming fast and furious, with everyone talking at the same time.

"Okay, everyone calm down," a commanding voice said from behind the high desk where the duty sergeant sat. "You men get back to your duties. I'll take care of this."

The whole room went suddenly quiet, and the uniformed officers who were hovering over me, firing questions, disappeared. I looked up and saw a tall, middle-aged man in the uniform of the county police, with captain's bars on his collars and a name tag that read SIMMONS. Beside him was a slightly younger man in a state police uniform. His name tag read KYLEY.

I started to stand, but the EMT pushed me back down into the chair. "Hold on there, Mr. Pennyback," he said. "I need to get this exit wound cleaned out and bandaged before it starts bleeding again. I don't know what the hell you put in it, but there's also danger of infection."

I already knew that, but infection was preferable to bleeding to death. But, I sat back in the chair and let him do his thing.

"That's all right . . . Mr. Pennyback, is it?" the captain said. I nodded. "I'm Captain Hank Simmons of the county police department, and this is Trooper John Kyley of the state police unit here in Oakland. You feel up to answering a few questions?"

I looked at the EMT who was kneeling beside my chair.

"He has a nasty gunshot wound in the leg, but seems okay otherwise," he said.

"Okay, captain," I said. "Fire away."

"Well, Mr. Pennyback, why don't we start with what the hell is a DC-based private investigator doing getting himself shot at in my county?"

I liked that. No beating around the bush. So, I told him everything. Well, not exactly everything. I left out the part about my client being the son of a former SS officer and probably in possession of a fortune of stolen art. That was a problem that was outside his jurisdiction, and one that I still hadn't decided how to handle. But, I did tell him about the Russians up in the hills with a local militia unit to whom they sold weapons. That got his attention. It got Kyley's attention too.

"You're telling us there are Russian mobsters in Garrett County, and they're hooked up with the militia?"

"Afraid so," I said. "If you look on the floor of the pickup I drove here in—which, I confess, I stole from them to get away—you'll find an AK-47 and two Glock 9mm pistols."

Simmons' eyes narrowed. "Your weapons or theirs?"

"Theirs," I said. "I don't own a firearm."

Now, both of them were looking at me suspiciously.

"If you don't have a gun, how'd you come by these three?" Kyley asked.

I then explained what had happened in the hills, and that unfortunately, they would find a dead Russian there.

Simmons ran a hand through his thinning hair.

"You took on four armed Russians, and not only got away from them and took their weapons, but you killed one with punji stakes?"

"I didn't intend to kill anyone. The booby trap was to slow them down so I'd have a chance of getting away. If they hadn't left him alone, he might have survived. I left two of them tied up in the cabin in that compound, but I imagine they're already planning their getaway."

Simmons spun on his heel and pointed at the desk sergeant who had been sitting listening open-mouthed. "Collins, call in all our off-duty officers and open the armory. Issue tactical gear and plenty of ammunition." To Kyley he said, "How many men you got in the state police barracks?"

"Accounting for the ones who're probably on patrol, I'd say about five to eight."

"Call 'em and have 'em suit up for a raid. Expect heavy resistance."

Kyley saluted and ran off. The EMT was just finishing up bandaging my thigh. I started to stand.

"Where do you think you're going,

Pennyback?" Simmons asked.

"I can show you the way to the militia compound," I said. "And, I have to retrieve the rental car I left in the forest."

"We won't need your directions. I know exactly where that damned compound is. We've been keeping an eye on those militia boys whenever they come down to town, but I had no idea they were doing arms deals up there. Look, I have no reason to doubt you're who you say you are, but until we confirm it, you're staying right here where my men can keep an eye on you. Besides, it's dark out there, and we'll have enough to do without having to look out for an unarmed civilian . . . even one able to defeat four armed men. Don't worry about your rental. When we've cleared that compound, I'll have someone go up and tow it to town for you."

Simmons was a man accustomed to giving orders, and I had no doubt that if I gave him any shit, I'd do my waiting in a holding cell, so I just nodded and sat back down. I gave him a rough description of where I'd left the 4-Runner, and he assured me he would take care of it.

As I sat back, he rushed off to meet Kyley coming through the front door, and several county police officers, some already in armored vests and helmets, coming from somewhere in the rear of the building.

"You'd better hurry," I said. "They'll have to know I contacted the authorities."

"Not to worry," Simmons said. "There's only one road out of that area, and we can get to where it connects with the highway from here quicker than they can. I can assure you, they're not getting away."

Well, not much I could say in response to that. As I sat back, I realized that I didn't really *want* to go with them. I just felt that it was necessary to make the offer, and I guess I was secretly glad Simmons had turned me down. I couldn't be sure about the militia, and I had no idea how many Russians were left at the compound, but there was likely to be some gunfire, and I *hate* night combat. I'm not fond of combat anytime, but getting shot in the dark's a real pisser.

Thinking of that reminded me that I really needed to go, so I asked the sole remaining cop in the station for directions to the john. After relieving myself, I came back, took a long drink of cold water from the fountain in the back of the room, got a bag of Cheetos and a Snickers Bar from the vending machine, ate them, and then went back to the semi-comfortable chair across from the desk sergeant and promptly fell asleep.

Chapter
Twenty-Nine

The thumping of boots on the hard floor, and clattering of weapons being stacked woke me up. I had a slight pain in my neck and a stiff back from the position I'd been in, sleeping on a straight-back chair.

I opened my eyes to see Simmons standing over me with his hands on his hips. His eyes were bloodshot and he had mud stains on his cheeks.

"Morning, sleeping beauty," he said. "You're finally back in the land of the living."

Groggy eyed, I looked at my watch. It was 5:15.

"Why didn't you wake me as soon as you got back," I said.

"We're just getting back." He looked completely beat. "Damn fools decided to put up a fight."

"I take it that didn't go too well with them."

He laughed. "Those militia boys go up in the hills and play soldier and they think they're pretty hot shit, but they were up against a pissed off bunch of county cops and state troopers who've been anxious to use some of the toys the Defense Department gave us after 9/11. It was pretty one-sided, and now they're residents in the county lockup, except for five who didn't duck in time . . . they're under guard in the hospital with bullets in their sorry hides."

"I hope none of your men were hurt," I said. "Did you catch the Russians?"

"We found the dead one just where you said he'd be and two others wandering lost in the woods. They didn't have much fight in 'em, but they don't speak English, so we're waiting for the FBI to show up with an interpreter." His brow wrinkled. "As for the two you said you left in the cabin, we found one, and from the description you gave I'd say it's this Viktor Ivanov fellow. He had a bullet hole in his forehead. There was no sign of this Kolchak guy. Oh, and we found your rental. It's outside in the parking lot."

So, I thought, Kolchak got loose first. I wouldn't shed any tears over Ivanov. I imagine that Kolchak realized that Ivanov would view his failure to kill me as a betrayal. I'd heard how the Russian mob dealt with disloyalty or failure, and I'd seen the callous way Kolchak had treated his men. It would have been better if Kolchak had been captured, but he was the lesser of two evils, and if one had to survive, I voted for him over Ivanov.

"Too bad," I said. "But, Ivanov was the brains behind the operation, so you should be happy you . . . or whoever . . . got him."

"I wish it was that easy. This'll shut down this one militia, but it won't be long before another one'll spring up to replace it. Same with the gun runners. Shit, it's like 'Whack-a-Mole,' you slap 'em down in one place and they pop up in another."

Sad, but true. Militias are an unfortunate fact of life, with a group for every flavor of belief, from survivalists to the crackpots who're convinced that the UN has an army poised to invade the country. With the country's love affair with guns, and lobbyists ensuring ineffective control over sales and ownership of all kinds of killing tools, there would be no shortage of people willing to sell to the next group, and, as Ivanov's presence testified, even foreign groups were willing to enter the marketplace.

I shook my head. "Yeah, I guess you're right. At least, you put this one out of business. And, thanks for retrieving my car."

"Not a problem." He looked at his watch. "Say, I know it's early for a city fellow, but how about some breakfast? There's a place a few blocks away that does steak and eggs."

At the mention of food, my stomach rumbled, reminding me that I hadn't eaten anything but junk food since the previous day's breakfast.

"It's never too early for breakfast," I said. "And, steak and eggs sound perfect."

"Great. Give me time to shuck this gear and we'll take my car."

Chapter
Thirty

By 5:45 Simmons and I were seated in a back booth of a place called Carla's Country Kitchen, which was a white version of Mom's in DC, with oil cloth table covers with red and white square patterns, napkins in twisted wire holders, and menus in plastic covers. The waitress was a skinny redhead with an overbite and knock-knees, with an accent that sounded like central casting had sent her to try out for a remake of 'The Beverly Hillbillies.' But, the food, heavy on fried dishes, was just what the doctor ordered. By 7:00, we were sitting back in our booths, rubbing our stomachs and enjoying a second cup of coffee.

"I need to make some phone calls," I said, after looking at my watch, and realizing that I was more than a day overdue, and Sandra and Heather, in that order, would be worried. "My girlfriend, my partner, and my buddy on the police force were expecting me home Saturday night, and it's now Monday morning."

"Can't help you with the girlfriend or partner," Simmons said. "But, if the cop friend's a detective named Mayweather, he knows you're okay."

"How's that?"

"You were pretty tired and beat up last night, but you mentioned his name a couple of times. I had my sergeant call DC, and we got hold of him around one this morning. My sergeant says he's a grumpy son of a bitch, but he vouched for you. Said you're a pain in the ass, but a pretty standup guy. He didn't seem at all surprised, I'm told, that you managed to take on four armed Russians and come out on the winning side."

I just shrugged. Simmons seemed like a nice enough guy, but I don't share things about myself easily, so a shrug seemed the safest way to respond. He just smiled knowingly.

"That just leaves my girlfriend and my partner, two of the toughest women in the world," I said. "I'd go up against Russians any day of the week rather than piss off either of them."

He held up his left hand and showed me his wedding ring. "I know what you mean. Well, let's get back to the office. You can call from there."

We did the obligatory tap dance over who'd pay the bill, but since my payday for this trip was a hell of a lot more than his salary, probably what he earned in a year in fact, I convinced him to let me pay. The redhead gave me a grin that was full of prominent teeth when I left a five dollar tip.

In the rush to get away, first from Kolchak and then from the militia, I'd neglected to turn my phone off and the battery was drained, so I had to take Simmons up on the use of his phone. He let me have the use of his office and direct line. The guy was coming closer to making my tentative friend list.

I called Sandra first, hoping to catch her before she left for school. I did.

"Al, babe," she said breathlessly. "Are you okay? Where the hell have you been? You were supposed to be home Saturday night?"

Her words came tumbling out in a torrent of concern. I assured her that I was okay—I decided to tell her about the gunshot wound in person—and would be home in a few hours. Then I gave her an abbreviated and highly censored version of the weekend's events. She's no fool, though. She knew that I was leaving things out.

"It wasn't a milk run, was it?" she asked.

I was busted. "I'll tell you all about it tonight," I said. "Promise."

I wasn't looking forward to that conversation.

My next call was to Heather. I called her mobile, but as soon as she answered, I knew that she was already in the office from the traffic sounds that were just barely audible over the phone.

"How bad was it?" she asked. She has the Caller ID function on her phone, and unlike me, knows how to use it. There wasn't much use trying to hold anything back from her either.

"Well, other than the fact that there was no painting, and I got shot in the leg, it wasn't all bad," I said.

There was a gasp at her end, and it didn't come from a car's exhaust pipe.

"You're joking, right? No, you're not joking. Okay, what the hell happened, and please start from the beginning." There was no indication of panic in her voice. Heather and I'd been through too much together for her to be too surprised at anything.

She wanted it from the beginning, so I gave it to her from the beginning. I ended it with a list of the things I needed her to start doing right away. "I want you to see if you can dig up anything on Kurt Richter. He would have been born in Germany, so he might not have a social security number, but maybe one of your contacts in Washington will be familiar with the name. While you're at it, see what you can find on an SS Captain Werner Richter. That's Kurt's father according to the Russian."

"You want me to look the Russians up as well?" she asked.

"Well, the big boss, Viktor Ivanov, is dead, someone put a bullet in his head, but you might see what you can find on a former Soviet Spetznas guy named Ivan Kolchak. I have a feeling he's been freelance muscle since the Soviet Union went kaput, so he might be on someone's radar screen."

"I doubt I'll have anything by the time you get back today, so you might as well go straight home and get some rest. Sounds like you need it."

Yeah, about 48 straight hours of rest, but I knew damn well I wouldn't be able to sleep until I solved the mystery that was Chester Boulware *nee* Kurt Richter.

This had started out as an over-compensated delivery job, but it had morphed into an overly-complicated mess. Stolen Nazi art, arms trafficking, right wing militia nuts, and Russian gangsters. It was enough to make me want a strong drink. But, that would have to wait until after I drove back to DC.

"I need you to meet me at the rental car agency to give me a ride home."

"No problem," she said. "Call me when you hit Germantown. That'll give me time to get there about the same time you do."

After she rang off, I debated calling Buster, but just as I was about to hit his number on speed dial, I had a brain flash. There was one person who might be able to get the information I needed even easier than Heather, and he wouldn't have to make but one phone call.

I scrolled down my list of phone contacts until I found the number. Then, I called Carlton Raine.

Chapter
Thirty-One

"Hey, young fellow," Raine's cultured voice came through the speaker. "What's got you calling me so early in the morning?"

Damn, even a senior citizen like Raine had Caller ID. I was going to have to break down and get me one of those smart phones—and learn how to use it.

"Sorry if I woke you up, Blood," I said.

"But, I need some help."

"You didn't wake me up, son. I've been up since five. At my age, I don't need as much sleep as I once did. What do you need?"

I told him. I could imagine him at the other end of the phone, looking as placid as if I was asking to borrow his lawn mower, not even blinking.

"I imagine you need this information right away," he said.

"As soon as you can get it; yesterday would be fine. Then, I have to decide what to do about it."

There was a long silence. "You still there?" I asked.

"Yeah, I'm still here. I was just writing things down. My memory's not what it used to be." I knew that to be a crock. Raine had the ability to retain huge amounts of information in his mind and recall it perfectly days later. "Okay, here's what I have. You want to know about Kurt Richter, son of a Nazi SS Capitan Werner Richter, and whether or not he's involved in the smuggling of art stolen by the Nazis during World War II."

"Not just during, but before as well."

"Yeah, I know that. This kind of thing is usually handled by the FBI working with Interpol, but the Russian connection and arms sales to U.S. militia will interest my friends out at Langley, so I'm sure I can find a snippet or two." Another pause. "You're driving down from Garrett County this morning, right?"

"Sure, I should be leaving here in a few minutes."

"Why don't you plan to come by and have lunch with me? I should have something for you by then."

That would work. I should have time to drive to Rockville, turn in the rental, let Heather drive me home, and I could clean the grit and grime off with a nice long shower before driving to his place.

` "Sounds like a plan," I said. "See you around noon."

After breaking the connection, I called Buster and Quincy, and gave them brief versions of what had happened, and what I planned to do. Buster offered to help me nail Richter, an offer I said I'd take into account, and Quincy sputtered apologies for getting me involved. He, too, said he would help me, attorney-client privileges be damned. It's good to have friends like that.

Charles Ray

Chapter
Thirty-Two

Despite it being my left leg that was injured, driving such a distance wasn't comfortable, forcing me to pull over and get out to stretch several times before I pulled into the rental car dealer's lot in Rockville at 10:30. I'd changed pants before leaving Oakland to avoid generating questions, but the clerk still eyed me strangely when I limped in favoring my left leg.

Heather was waiting for me, and other than eying me sympathetically when she thought I wasn't looking, wisely kept her mouth shut until she dropped me off in front of my house.

"I'll plan to see you tomorrow," she said as I got out of the car. "Take care of that leg."

"Okay, kid," I said. "Call me on my cell if you learn anything interesting."

I stood there and watched as she drove away. Then, I went inside and spent twenty minutes in the shower. The bandage on my leg got soaked, but the hot soapy water felt so good, I ignored it and dried it off with Sandra's hair dryer after I'd toweled off. Refreshed at last, and in clean clothes, I got in the Bug and drove to Raine's house.

After greeting me on the porch, he led me into the living room.

"I thought we'd use TV trays and sit on the couch," he said. "I made breaded pork chops and red beans with a bit of rice on the side. Hope you don't mind."

Mind? He had to be kidding. The thought of the food, combined with the aroma drifting in from his kitchen had my mouth watering.

"Sounds fine to me." I sat on the sofa.

He went into the kitchen and came back a few minutes later carrying a TV tray in each hand. After handing me one and putting the other one on the coffee table, he went back to the kitchen. He was back quickly with a large pitcher of iced tea and two tumblers.

"Iced tea with no sugar, just the way you like it," he said.

A lot of people like to talk while they eat, but in the southern culture that Raine and I were raised in, the act of eating is not sullied with words, at least not at first. The food is the reason you gather around a table, and it's to the food you pay homage, until the initial hunger pangs are satisfied.

We were using our forks to push the remaining rice around to sop up what was left of the beans before he finally looked over at me.

"Okay, youngster," he said. "You want to know what I found out about your German friend, right? Well, hold onto your seat, because this will knock your socks off."

I paused with a forkful of rice, bean juice dripping off, halfway to my mouth. "Don't tell me . . . he's a neo-Nazi."

"No, nothing so pedestrian." He laughed. "His father, Werner, was a real jackboot, a hardcore SS type, but Kurt, is into more sophisticated crime, according to Interpol."

I put my fork down, food now forgotten.

"Whoa! This guy's wanted by Interpol? How the hell did he get into the U.S.? What's he wanted for?"

He held his hands up like a traffic cop. "That's a lot of questions, but let me see if I can answer them all." He began ticking things off on his fingers. "First, he's wanted by the police in England, Germany, Austria, and Belgium, which is why Interpol's interested. It seems his father, who managed to get out of Germany with young Kurt and his mother right after the war, also took a lot of stolen art with him. They got to Argentina, along with a lot of other Germans, but the trail went cold there about thirty years ago. Word on the street is that when his father and mother died, Kurt kept the business going, and got himself involved in art theft big time. As to how he got into this country, the guys out at Langley would like to know that, and I imagine so would the FBI and Homeland Security."

"This, of course, is assuming that Boulware really is Kurt Richter. I only have the word of a Russian gangster, and he's dead now."

"There is that, of course," he said. "If it turns out that he is Richter, what do you plan to do?"

I hadn't thought it out that far. I suppose the right thing to do was report it to the authorities. The problem would be deciding *who* the proper authorities would be. If the guy was indeed an international criminal, the FBI would be the most logical agency to deal with it, but with the shakeup since 9/11 and the creation of the Department of Homeland Security, I wasn't sure any more who did what. I had no desire to get caught up in some jurisdictional squabble.

"I'll cross that bridge when I come to it," was the only answer I could give him. "In the meantime, I have nearly a million dollars of his money, and I suppose I'll have to arrange to return it to him."

He laughed. It was funny when I thought of it. Here I was, having just discovered that my client was ion all likelihood some big time international art thief, and I was worrying about how to dispose of the money he'd entrusted to me. Money that was intended to buy a famous piece of stolen art that a lot of people on both sides of the Atlantic would have given their left nuts to get their hands on at that. That was another complication. If I went to the feds, they were just as likely to accuse me of being complicit in an illegal transaction.

All this started with me doing a favor for a friend. No good deed goes unpunished.

Charles Ray

Chapter
Thirty-Three

Back home I hadn't even had time to put my car keys away when the phone rang. It was Buster.

"Hey, bro," he said. "Why haven't you called me today?" He sounded a little put out.

"Oh, hey, Buster, I was just about to do that. You know how it is. I had to check in with Sandra and Heather first." I left out that I'd also talked to Blood Raine before him. He'd probably think that was some kind of violation of the Bro Code, a kick he'd gotten into in the previous several months that I still did not understand.

"Okay, I guess I can see that." His tone sounded mollified, not completely satisfied, but no longer miffed. "How'd Sandra take your getting shot?"

"Uh . . . I only talked to her on the phone. She was already off to work by the time I turned in my rental car and got a ride home. I thought I'd save that conversation for when we're face to face."

"Yeah, I can relate to that. Listen, I just wanted to let you know we got a preliminary report back on the prints on that briefcase you gave me."

"That's great. What's the name and what's he wanted for?"

Long silence. I mean a real *long* silence. When Buster finally did speak, there was a hint of steel in his voice, that tone I'd seen him use on suspects who weren't answering his questions truthfully.

"What's going on, bro? You know something you ain't telling me?"

"Hey, no bullshit, amigo," I said. "I told you all I knew about this when we met at Mom's, and when I gave you that briefcase. I had a client who wasn't appearing in any databases, and I wanted to find out why."

"Yeah, I know all that, but then you go and get yourself shot by some Russian gangster and tangle up with some redneck militia dudes. I know *something* more than you told me is going on, so spill, or I don't tell you what I know."

Buster can be a real hard ass when he sets his mind to it, and I did owe him a bit more explanation than I'd previously given. So, I brought him up to date on what I knew.

His tone, when he spoke again, was edging back toward mollified territory.

"Okay, that explains what the feds found," he said. "The prints you gave me belong to some cat named Kurt Richter. He's not wanted for anything here, but the cops in several European countries have warrants out for him for art theft, dealing in stolen art, and art forgery."

"Well, that fits with what I learned from the Russians."

"This client of yours, Chester Boulware, he's Kurt Richter?"

"Looks like it."

"So, what do you plan to do?"

Good question. On the one hand, if I didn't want to jeopardize my PI license, I would have to notify the authorities. But, that left me with a case full of money to dispose of. I suppose the thing to do was turn that over too, but just handing three quarters of a million over to federal cops grated on me.

"What do you suggest?" I asked.

"You know you have to inform the authorities."

"I have, amigo. You're a DC cop and I just told you what I suspect."

"Hold up, bro," he said. "I'm a DC cop, true, but this is way outside my jurisdiction."

"Couldn't you tell the feds you got the information from an anonymous informant or something? I mean, they have to be curious about where you got the fingerprints, right?"

"That's putting it mildly. My captain's been asking me about that ever since the report came in . . . I couldn't hide it from him. I already used the confidential informant story, but I'm not sure he's buying it. Everyone here in the precinct knows about my relationship with you, and this kind of shit has your name all over it."

I knew that if I asked him to do it, Buster would risk the wrath of his superiors in order to cover for me, but I wasn't willing to go that far.

"Okay, you go ahead and tell them where you got the briefcase, and that I suspect my client is actually Kurt Richter, a wanted man."

"That's a smart move, Al," he said. "I wouldn't want to see you risking your license for this crap."

"Not to worry. I'll take care of things on my end. I'll talk to you later."

Before he could ask what I meant by 'taking care of things,' I broke the connection.

Knowing how the system works, I figured that by the time Buster finished briefing his boss, who would then have to brief *his* boss, and then the information would get passed to someone in the federal bureaucracy who would go through the whole brief the chain of command thing, it would be several hours before anyone actually made a move on Boulware/Richter. That gave me enough time to do what I had to do.

Charles Ray

Chapter
Thirty-Four

I pulled up to the iron gates at 3:05 and announced myself. There was a brief pause and then the gates swung open. This time, I parked directly in front of the main entrance. No way was I hoofing it all the way from the parking lot to the house lugging the weight of all that money.

The butler gave me a strange look when he opened the door, but stepped aside to allow me to enter. He didn't offer to take the case. I wouldn't have given it to him anyway. I walked through the door and turned to go to the room where I'd previously met Richter—I still found it hard to think of the fat man by his real name—but the butler made a throat clearing sound.

"The master is waiting for you in the main salon," he said, and pointed down the hallway to the left.

The long, wide hallway was a twin to the other side, with expensive looking statues and vases on polished wooden stands and even more expensive looking paintings adorning both walls. At the far end was an archway through which I could see an expanse of beige marble floor and a white marble wall that looked like it was a football field length from the archway.

"Through the archway?" I asked.

He made a sniffing noise. "Of course," he said. He turned and walked toward the back of the house down a shorter hallway, also with paintings on both walls, into a dimly lit room whose details I couldn't make out.

So much for service, I thought, adjusting the heavy canvas case on my shoulder, and heading toward the archway. This time, though, I paid attention to the artwork, especially the paintings. I didn't think Richter would be stupid enough to display Nazi stolen art on the walls, but he was a dealer in stolen artwork, so there was a good chance at least some, if not all, the pictures were stolen. There were at least twenty paintings on the walls of the hallway, probably worth millions of dollars. Of course, they could also be counterfeits or cheap originals for all I knew. It would have been helpful to have Sandra there, with her knowledge of art.

Oh well, I thought, best let the feds worry about it when they finally came to get Richter.

I finally reached the archway. I stopped and looked inside the huge room. It was sparsely furnished, lots of mahogany, metal, and leather, and the walls, like the hallway, were covered with dozens of paintings, large and small. The guy was living in a damn art museum.

After making one last adjustment of the strap over my shoulder, I stepped through the archway.

Richter was sitting on a large black leather sofa off to the right, near the center of the room. He'd looked large in the study, but for some reason, he looked even larger in the much larger space. He covered the center cushion and half of each cushion on either side, looking like an oversized Buddha statue draped in a lime green dressing gown that reached the floor, leaving only his oversized feet to show beneath the hem. He looked up and smiled when I entered. Raising a fat hand, he waved me forward like some ancient potentate summoning a servant.

I stopped six feet from the sofa. There were two matching black leather chairs facing the sofa. He pointed to the one on the right.

"Have a seat, Mr. Pennyback," he said. "Refreshments will be served shortly."

"That's okay, I'll stand. I won't be here long. I'm afraid I have bad news."

"The offer was a ruse. There was no painting."

It wasn't a question. He knew.

"That's right, but how did you know?"

"I saw it on the morning news," he said. "A shootout between a militia gang and the police in Garrett County, and two dead men believed to be Russian. I also noticed that you were limping when you walked in. Your name wasn't mentioned in the news, but it would have to be a coincidence for your limp and this battle not to be related, and I do not believe in coincidences." His eyes stayed on the case on my shoulder as he spoke, and his pudgy fingers beat tattoos on the tops of his thighs.

"You don't seem surprised at any of this," I said.

His fingers stopped tapping and he looked briefly at me before shifting his gaze back to the case.

"In the art world it happens sometimes

that unscrupulous people will try to pass off forgeries."

"Yeah, but this wasn't a case of trying to sell you a forged painting. The guy didn't have a painting to sell. He seemed more interested in meeting *you* face to face."

His piggy little eyes blinked rapidly. The fingers started their drumming again. I could see little beads of sweat in the folds of flesh of his jaws and neck.

"Ah, yes, that is strange," he said. "But, I *am* a well-known figure in the art world. Perhaps he wanted to make an even more lucrative deal and he used this ruse to get to me."

Yeah, and I own some prime real estate in the Florida swamps that I'll let you have cheap. I didn't need the non-verbal indicators to know he was lying; that wasn't even close to a good lie.

"It didn't seem that way to me. It sounded like what he wanted to do was get close to you so he could kill you."

He squeezed his eyes shut, opened them, and fixed me with a steely stare as he raised his hands and brought them together and rested the bump of flesh under his lips that passed for his chin on them. "Ah, I am truly sorry that Mr. Ivanov, in his ire at me, sent his ruffians to shoot at you."

"I never mentioned the name Ivanov, and I certainly didn't say anything about being shot at."

He blinked again. "Uh, I must have heard it on the news."

I had the fat bastard. Finally, I'd caught him in a lie that I could pin him with. "I don't think so. I doubt the cops would have released Ivanov's name to the media this early, since they hadn't the means in Garrett County to positively ID him, and I *know* damn well they kept me out of it entirely. So, the question Mr. Boulware . . . or should I call you *Herr* Richter . . . is how the hell you know this?"

I heard a whisper of sound on the marble floor behind me. I turned slowly, and the answer to my question stood there just inside the room with a nasty looking black Makorov 9mm pistol pointed at me.

"Good afternoon, Mr. Pennyback," Kolchak said. "So nice to see you again."

Chapter
Thirty-Five

I tightened my grip on the strap across my shoulder, at the same time keeping a wary eye on the deadly automatic pistol in Kolchak's hand.

"I wish I could say the same for you," I said. "I guess you got out of that rope before your boss, or I should say your *late* boss. I must say, though, I'm surprised to see you here."

"It is just fortunate that I was able to get out of my bonds before Ivanov, or I would be dead instead of him. Thank you, by the way, for binding me to the desk. It rubbed my legs raw, but thanks to its weight, I was able to loosen the rope and free myself. As for my being here, I can no longer return to Russia. I needed employment, and from what I learned from Ivanov, this appears to be where my special skills can be put to more lucrative use."

I turned to Richter.

"You hired him?"

Richter smiled and nodded, setting the flesh of his jowls to quivering. "It seemed like a good business decision. He has skills that I can put to use on occasion, and knowledge that is even more valuable."

"A Russian working for a German, now that's a marriage made in hell," I said to Kolchak.

"Money is more important than ideology," he said. "Just look at your American toy soldiers. They are very right wing, but they do not mind doing business with former Communists if the price is right. I needed a job, and this man made an offer that was attractive."

"You do know that this man's the son of a Nazi, and is probably a neo-Nazi himself, right?"

Out of the corner of my eye I saw Richter's

eyes widen.

"So, Mr. Pennyback, you've been checking up on me, have you? What do you think you know?"

"I know that your name's really Kurt Richter, and that your father was SS Captain Werner Richter, for starters."

"How very resourceful and perceptive of you. Imagine you learned this from the late Viktor Ivanov?"

I saw no point in alerting him that I'd learned of him through international police sources, and that the feds were probably just hours away from descending upon his estate. I didn't like the way he was looking at me, though. The way he sat there, almost unblinking, looking at me like a big bullfrog eying a tasty dragon fly.

"Yeah, he knew all about you . . . well, almost everything." I didn't want to piss him off by referring to his weight. "In fact, this whole deal was set up so he could get close to you and kill you."

"Yes, I am aware of that, thanks to Mr. Kolchak here." He looked at the case on my shoulders. "Thanks to your resourcefulness, though, I did not lose my money."

"I'm a bit curious, though," I said, changing the subject. "How did Kurt Richter, wanted international art thief, get into the U.S. without being noticed?"

"My, my, it sounds like you and Viktor had quite the chat. If you must know, I never did like living in Argentina, so when my father died, I relocated to Venezuela, and made my way to the United States by boat. Two decades ago, it you had enough money, and I had more than enough from selling the paintings my father was able to smuggle out of Germany and the money we'd made after moving to Argentina, you could hire a vessel that was capable of slipping past your Coast Guard and landing on an isolated shore. From there, I hired people to bring me here to Washington. What better place to hide than right under the noses of the people looking for you; the one place they never seem to look."

That was before the events of September 11, 2001, of course, when drug smugglers and Cuban refugees were the main travelers slipping in by boat. I imagined that Richter had chartered a luxury yacht that had all the proper paperwork, just in case they were stopped, although how they hid someone as large as him, I couldn't even guess.

"And, you've lived here all this time and never come to the attention of the authorities?"

"Never once. To my neighbors I'm must a rich recluse who never leaves his house. The holding company my father established years ago is used to pay for everything, so there has been no need for me to show my face. Sums of cash to meet my immediate needs are brought in periodically by couriers who are quite experienced in evading your Customs authorities."

Then, a thought hit me. He was telling me his secrets, secrets he'd kept hidden for decades. There could only be one reason for that. He planned for me to take his secrets to my grave—and soon.

"I suppose you're telling me this because you don't expect me to tell the authorities."

"Precisely, Mr. Pennyback. You are, as I said, quite perceptive, and from what Quincy Chang says about you, honest to a fault. You've proven that by bringing my money back. Unfortunately, that also means you will feel obligated to tell the authorities what you know about me, and I simply cannot allow that."

"Just how do you propose to stop me?" Dumb question. I knew the answer, but I wanted to hear him say it.

"Why, by having Mr. Kolchak kill you."

Charles Ray

Chapter
Thirty-Six

I turned my attention back to Kolchak, who
had moved from his position near the
archway, and was now standing about ten
feet away with the Makarov aimed at my
center of mass. Unlike Richter, who had
porcine brown eyes that were sunk deep in

the fleshy folds of his face, Kolchak had blue eyes that were wide set in a face that was all angles. Like Richter's, though, his eyes were also lifeless. They were like two balls of glacier ice. They reflected the feelings he had inside—none. This was a man who killed for a living. I don't think he particularly enjoyed it. I don't think he gave a damn one way or another. To him it was just what he did.

:"You know, if you kill me here, someone's likely to hear the shot and call the police," I said.

"The house is relatively well soundproofed," Richter countered. "And, it's far enough from the street or any of my neighbors that it's likely not to be noticed."

"Besides, this is Makorov," Kolchak chimed in. "It will only make 'pop' sound. Someone hear, they maybe not even know it is a gun shooting, *da*."

"But, when they find my body and they learn that I've been shot with the same weapon used to kill Ivanov, they will become suspicious." This I said to Richter. He smiled.

"He is correct Herr Kolchak. That would then involve me. That is not good."

"No worries, Mr. Richter. You have car with large boot? I can make body disappear."

"Yes, I have several cars in fact. Take whichever one fits your requirements."

I was beginning to feel like a rabbit trapped in a cul de sac by a pack of hungry wolves.

"You're forgetting one thing," I said. "People

know I was coming here to meet you today. If I just disappear, there will be questions."

Kolchak's brow wrinkled, and he looked at Richter. Hah, I thought, hadn't thought about that one huh? But, Richter only smiled.

"He makes a good point, Herr Kolchak," he said. "Perhaps it would be better if you took him away in his own car. It will need to be removed from the premises anyway, and this way, my neighbors will see him drive away, should the authorities ever inquire."

I truly hate it when the bad guy is thinking one step ahead. Granted, Richter wasn't your ordinary bad guy. He'd managed to elude the authorities in several countries for decades, becoming filthy rich in the process, and had lived in luxury right under the noses of the FBI. If anyone should be able to outsmart me, it was him. It still rankled, though. In my world the good guys are supposed to win.

"This is good idea," Kolchak said, nodding in agreement. "I can make body and car disappear at the same time."

"Aren't you worried that your manservant might blab?" I asked Richter.

"Not in the least. He is well compensated for his discretion, well compensated indeed."

Kind of figured, really. It's almost impossible to keep secrets from household help. So, no help from the butler. In fact, I was quickly running out of options .

"My best friend's a DC cop, and he knows I

came here to return your money. He'll start asking questions if I disappear."

"That would be bad for him, bad indeed. If he asks the wrong questions in the wrong places, he too can be made to . . . disappear."

This guy was starting to *really* piss me off. It was one thing for him to have put me in jeopardy, but now he was making not so veiled threats against my friends, and you just don't do that. If his neck wasn't so thick, assuming he even had a neck under all the folds of fat, I would have liked nothing better than to wrap my hands around it and squeeze until he turned purple. But, the most immediate threat was standing in front of me with the business end of a Makarov pointing at my chest. Kolchak was just a hired gun whose services were available to the highest bidder. Killing me wouldn't be personal to him, just business. Of course, I'd be just as dead, so I couldn't afford to ignore him. Richter wasn't going anywhere, or at least he wouldn't be going very fast. It would take him a lot of time and effort just to heave his bulk up off the couch.

So, I decided to ignore him for the moment.

"What about you, Kolchak?" I asked, turning my attention to the threat that had to be neutralized if I was to survive. "Richter here is off the grid, but I gave your name and description to the cops in Garrett County. No doubt, they've notified the FBI, and there's a nationwide APB out for you as we speak."

He blinked. The first sign of emotion he'd shown since entering the room. I decided to turn the screw a little tighter.

"You think Richter's gonna risk his cushy little setup to protect you? Hell, you're just another tool he'll discard the moment it's no longer useful."

His gaze darted toward the fat man, and his expression wasn't pleasant.

"Do not let him manipulate you," Richter said. "He is just trying to delay the inevitable. Get him out of here and get rid of him. I am paying you well for your services."

"Whatever he's paying you is just pocket change to him, Kolchak. If the cops get you, he'll deny he ever saw you. I'll bet you he's paying you in cash, right?" Kolchak blinked again, which was just as good as a 'yes.' "No way to trace it back to him either. Bet he gave it to you in an envelope. He probably never touched it, so his prints won't be on it. You get caught, and you'll be hanging out all by your lonesome."

He blinked again.

"Enough of this nonsense," Richter snapped. "Do what I paid you to do, and there will be more, much more."

Kolchak didn't blink at that. I didn't need a map to see what was going on inside that block-shaped head of his. The man was nothing but a mercenary, his services available to the highest bidder, and Richter was the highest bidder in the room. I'd played all but one card in my weak deck. The final card was perhaps the weakest of all, but it was my last one to play. At moments like that, hesitation will get you killed. Acting would also in all likelihood get me killed, but when life's dealt you a weak hand, you have no choice but to play it. There would be no folding in this game.

I tensed my left arm and let the strap start to slide off my shoulder, gripping the top edge of the case tightly. When I felt the full weight of all that money in my hand, I dipped my left shoulder slightly, swung my hand back an inch, and then heaved forward with as much strength as I could muster. The pain in my left thigh hindered me, but only a bit. The laws of physics took charge, and the heavy case flew through the air toward Kolchak.

Humans are hardwired to wince and blink when a threat approaches them. It only takes a fraction of a second, but that fraction of a second is a lifetime when you're that close to death.

Kolchak flinched and his eyes closed as the case approached him. His gun hand dropped so that the Makarov was no longer pointed at me. It was only a fraction of a second, though, and he quickly recovered and brought the gun back up, squeezing the trigger as he did so. The gun made a popping noise, and *I* flinched, expecting to feel the white-hot sensation of a bullet. I was moving to the right, putting my weight on my right foot. In that very short moment, I realized that I hadn't felt a bullet hit me.

Everything was a blur, but my training and instincts had taken over. I stopped my motion to the right, planted my weight on my left foot, ignoring the pain shooting up my thigh, and brought my right foot up and around in a swinging kick in the direction of his head. The heel of my boot caught him in the temple, stunning him. I followed up with a right jab at the same spot, my knuckle, swollen from hours of punching the heavy bag and a hemp rope wrapped around a four by four board, contacted with his temple in the same spot my heel had hit. His eyes rolled back in their sockets and he went over backwards like a falling tree, unconscious before his head cracked against the marble floor, and his arms splayed out at his sides. The Makarov slid from his limp fingers, coming to a stop a foot from his outstretched fingers. The money-filled case was draped across his chest, but he wasn't complaining. He was out cold.

I whirled around and saw Richter pushing his fat hands against the cushions of the couch, attempting to rise.

I didn't think hitting him anywhere on the body would do much harm. Too much fat cushioning his body. So, I stepped forward, again ignoring the pain in my left leg, and snap kicked him in the forehead with my right foot. He sighed and sank back down on the couch, his head lolling to the side.

Two down, and I didn't have any extra holes in my body. Not a bad outcome for a plan that had only a snowball's chance in hell of working.

I took a deep breath and started to turn.

"Get down on your knees and put your hands on top of your head," a gruff voice said.

Chapter
Thirty-Seven

I had a momentary panic attack, thinking I'd miscounted the threats in the house and was now in a world of hurt. As I sank to my knees and started raising my hands, I was also doing a rapid-fire assessment of all the things I could do to get myself out of this situation, and came up with exactly—zero. Fortunately, the next voice I heard allowed me to ratchet the feeling of panic back to just feeling stupid kneeling there like a drug dealer who didn't run fast enough when the narcs yelled, 'raid.'

"That's okay, fellas, he's one of the good guys," Buster said in that booming voice of his. "Hey, bro, you can get up off your knees."

I made sure to keep my hands in plain view as I rose slowly to a standing position, and then turned around just as slowly. Buster, a wide smile on his dark brown face, stood in the doorway. He carried a Colt M4 assault rifle and was in full SWAT gear, complete with armored vest with POLICE in large white letters across his chest and a visored helmet. Beside him were two youngish looking guys armed and dressed similarly with FBI on their vests. The two FBI guys stopped pointing their M4s at me, but kept them ready to rectify that should Buster be wrong and I turned out to be one of the 'bad' guys. The one on Buster's left looked like he hoped that would be the case.

Buster looked around, first at me, and then at the two unconscious bodies, one on the floor and one on the couch, then shouldered his rifle and strode forward, grabbing my shoulders with his ham-sized hands.

"Bro, you got to stop having all the fun before we arrive," he said. He turned to the antsy FBI agent. "Maybe you ought to get that pistol off the floor and secure it in an evidence bag, don't you think, and I know these dudes are out cold, but it might be a good idea to cuff 'em anyway."

Neither of the agents looked happy at being ordered around by a local cop, but Buster made sense, so they complied.

"Glad you're here," I said. "But, you could have come earlier. I almost couldn't take these two down."

"Shit, Al, I seen you take on more'n this on an off day." He looked at Richter. "And, the fat dude don't look like he'd be dangerous unless he fell on you."

I could see the two FBI agents taking our conversation in.

"How'd you know I'd be here, anyway?" I asked.

"Because, bro, I know you. You're not the kind to let things lie. 'Sides, I knew you still had this dude's money, and you'd want to return it. Where is, by the way?"

I pointed to the case the FBI agent had lugged off Kolchak's body. "Turns out money's good for more than buying things," I said.

The agent turned the bag over. As he did so, I saw a hole in it. I didn't need to be told what that was. Despite being thrown off balance, Kolchak had still been a good shot. The placement of the round in that bag was about where my chest would have been if I hadn't thrown it at him.

"Money might not buy happiness," the FBI man said. "But, this money probably saved your life."

The other agent was struggling to move Richter's body to put zip ties on him. "I'm assuming this tub of lard is Kurt Richter," he said. "But, who's the guy on the floor?"

I briefly explained Kolchak's status. He whistled. "Damn, a Russian mobster and a neo-Nazi art thief." His eyes lit up. "This is turning into some bust."

"When you check his gun," I said. "I think you're gonna find it'll be the weapon that killed the dead Russian the authorities found in Garrett County."

"The SAIC briefed us on that this morning just before Detective Mayweather called," he said. "You mean this is connected to that?"

"It is, and I'll bet you your next paycheck when you check the art on the walls of this house, you'll find a lot of it's stolen."

His eyes went wide. His partner whistled. I could see they were both thinking promotions out of this.

"Damn, Al, you just keep falling into shit piles and coming up smelling like roses," Buster said. "First, you play the Russians and the militia for fools, and then you come down here and nail this bastard."

The FBI agents stopped what they were doing. Antsy was now looking at me with something approaching awe. "You were involved in the action up in Garrett County?"

"Damn straight he was," Buster said. "Al here disarmed four Russians who were chasing him through the woods, and then hogtied their boss and escaped a whole bunch of pissed off militia guys. Chief of police up there said, thanks to Al, they shut down a major arms smuggling ring."

They just shook their heads and continued to stare at me like they were fans and I was a rock star who'd just stepped from his limo and waved at them. I guess they were too new to the bureau to have heard of the incident when I'd been forced to shoot a rogue FBI agent who was mixed up with a smuggling ring.

"Actually, I spent most of the time just running, trying to keep from getting shot."

Buster clapped me on the shoulder, rocking me forward. "Don't listen to him. He's just bein' modest. This dude's the real deal. I seen him go up against a militia group in West Virginia once, and he never even carries a piece, just kicks the shit out of 'em with that kung fu stuff."

"It's actually taekwondo," I said.

"Whatever," he said. "Old Al here just goes all Bruce Lee on perps and they fall like bowling pins."

I didn't have to heart to correct him any further. Bruce Lee was a gifted martial artist, but the stuff he did in the movies would only get you killed in a real fight—and most of it was impossible anyway without special effects. And, that 'woo-o-o' sound he made when fighting; well, let's just say, in a real fight, except maybe yelling when you first attack to throw your opponent off, you don't have town for crap like that. You save your breath so your lungs can pump oxygen to your heart and muscles.

"I think I've read about you in the *Washington Post*," the FBI agent standing near Richter said. "You've solved some pretty big cases. You're some kind of Robin Hood to the common folks of the area, or something like that?"

He'd obviously either not read the paper carefully, or his memory was for shit. Lucy Garcia, a features reporter for the *Post*, had been following my activity for years, ever since I solved the murder of a young inner city student that the police had mistakenly attributed to gang activity. She'd been so impressed with the fact that I was willing to work for people who wouldn't normally be able to afford to hire a private investigator, and who often, unfortunately, got very little attention from the police, she'd dubbed me the Brown Knight. Heather kept her informed of our cases, without violating client confidentially, and sometimes they were just the type of things that you couldn't keep quiet, and she did a piece about every two or three months. I wasn't a Robin Hood. None of that stealing from the rich for me. But, I didn't have the heart to correct him.

"You can't believe everything you read in the paper," I said. "I solve the occasional hard case, but I'm no miracle worker. Just lucky mostly."

Buster smacked my shoulder again. "Well, pardner, you just keep on being lucky, and we'll keep locking the mothers up."

The FBI agent still looked awed. "Damn, I wish I had your luck."

Charles Ray

Chapter
Thirty-Eight

When Richter came to and found himself zip-tied and his home being pulled apart by FBI agents, he shot me a murderous glare. One of the FBI agents who'd come in with Buster, I'd learned that his name was—I kid you not—

Henry Doolittle, was standing over him with a note pad and pen in hand.

"Are you Kurt Richter?" he asked.

Richter looked up at him with the look you'd give a puppy that has just pissed on your best carpet. *"Ich verstehen nicht,"* he said.

So, he was going to play it that way, I thought. 'I don't understand,' indeed. It didn't impress Doolittle either.

"Actually, *Herr* Richter, I think you do understand," he said. "In fact, *ich denke sie alles verstandig.* Or would you prefer me to conduct this interview in German? French? Spanish perhaps? All languages I'm aware that you're quite fluent in . . . as well as English. We can get an interpreter for any or all of them."

That took the wind out of Richter. He seemed to shrink two whole sizes before my eyes. Of course, that still left him as big as two of me. Doolittle looked down at him with an expression of smug satisfaction.

"I . . . do not wish to say anything until my lawyer is present," Richter said finally.

"You mean Quincy Chang, right?" I asked.

He continued to glare at me, but nodded.

"You can call him once we've booked you," Doolittle said.

I smiled at the agent. "It might be interesting to let him do it right now," I said, pulling my cell phone from my pocket. "In fact, I can get him on the phone."

Doolittle looked momentarily confused. He looked intently at me, and must have seen something in my expression, because he smiled and nodded.

"Okay, I don't see why not," he said. "Everyone's entitled to legal representation."

I hit Quincy's number on speed dial and then put my phone on speaker. The beeping sound, followed by the metallic ringing echoed off the marble walls.

"Holcombe, Stein and Chang, Mr. Chang's office, how may I help you?" Quincy's personal assistant, a woman of indeterminate age, ever-changing hair color, and a penchant for flirting with me, sounded sexier and younger over the phone than I knew her to be in real life.

"May I speak to Mr. Chang, please? I have his client, Mr. Boulware here, and he wishes to speak with him," I said.

She put me on hold, thankfully without the annoying elevator music that usually accompanies that action. In a few seconds, Quincy's cultured voice came out of the little speaker.

"Quincy Chang here," he said. "Mr. Boulware, what is it you wish to speak with me about."

Richter looked around, as if waiting for us to leave the room and give him some privacy. The law provides for attorney-client privacy, even for people under arrest, but no one made a move to leave.

"Just tell him to meet you at our Washington field office," Doolittle said, giving him the address. I held the phone near Richter's face.

"I take it you heard that, Quincy," Richter said. "I'm being arrested by the FBI. I need you to meet me there to arrange my immediate release."

Quincy cleared his throat. "I'm afraid, Mr. Boulware . . . or should I call you Mr. Richter? Anyway, this firm no longer represents you. Information has come to us that indicates you retained our services under false pretenses. Our contract, therefore, is null and void. In addition, we do not do criminal cases. I'd be happy to recommend a good criminal defense lawyer if you wish."

Richter got the glassy-eyed look of a cornered animal, one that knows it's dead even if it is still breathing.

"Y-you cannot do this to me. I have p-paid quite a substantial retainer to—"

"Your entire retainer for this month will be returned," Quincy said, cutting him off. "Should I have my assistant make the check out to Chester Boulware or Kurt Richter, or perhaps I should just send it to Phoenix Corporation?"

Richter looked up at me. I kept my expression neutral despite the fact that I was enjoying the hell out of seeing him squirm like a frog on a gig. His gaze darted to the others, first the FBI agents, then Buster. They just looked back at him with the same look I'm sure they'd given hundreds, if not thousands, of times before to the perps they'd slapped the cuffs on. The message Richter was getting was loud and clear, 'screw you, you're busted.' The fat man looked like he wanted to cry.

I pulled the phone away. "I don't think Mr. Richter has anything else to say, Quincy."

"Fine," Quincy said. "I'm busy now anyway. But, while I have you on the phone, I want to apologize for getting you involved in this mess."

"Hey, Quince, don't be apologizing," Buster said in a loud voice. "If you hadn't hooked Al up with this dirt bag we might not have ever known he was hiding out here in DC. You did a solid, man."

"Thanks, Buster, you too, Al. You've facilitated getting this firm out of a potentially damaging, and certainly unsavory situation. I owe you both."

"We'll collect later, amigo," I said, and broke the connection. I turned to the FBI agents. "Well, looks like he won't be talking to his lawyer so soon after all. He'll have to find a new lawyer, and I'm willing to bet that no reputable firm in this town will take him on as a client. He'll either have to hire a low-rent shyster or let the court appoint a public defender."

Somehow, the thought of someone who'd

lived in such luxurious surroundings having to be represented by a public defender was funny, and we started laughing. Well, all of us except Richter. He just sat back on the couch and glared at us.

Kolchak started coming around about this time. Unlike Richter, he accepted his fate stoically. He probably considered anything American law enforcement would throw at him would be mild compared to what he'd face back in Mother Russia. The feds would probably turn him over to the state of Maryland for the murder of Ivanov, unless they wanted to prosecute him on the federal gun running charges first. Maryland has the death penalty, but it's not as quick to impose it as its neighbors to the south, so he might escape the needle if—when—convicted. But, he'd be behind bars for a long, long time.

As for Richter, well, the rich have their own subset of the justice system, one in which they tend to skate or get an easy ride for things that get us common folks hard time, but I had a feeling his Nazi connections, and the embarrassment the government would be feeling about how he'd played them for so long would cancel out some of that privilege. Even if he didn't get whacked by the U.S. system, several European countries would be lining up to demand his extradition, and I imagine Germany would be leading the pack. His heritage would get him no sympathy there.

No, both of them would get what they deserved in one form or another. And, I'd successfully closed another case and racked up some more credits with both local and federal law enforcement. Heather would be ecstatic, and Lucy would probably get the whole front page of the style section with this one.

I put my phone back in my pocket.

"Is it okay if I go home now?" I asked. "My leg's bumming me, and I need to get some rest. I have a really stressful job to do tonight."

The FBI agents looked at me, perplexed expressions contorting their faces. Buster looked momentarily confused, and then broke out into a broad grin. "You still haven't told her, have you?"

"I haven't seen her yet. I didn't want to tell her over the phone."

"Man, she's gonna be royally pissed."

"Don't I know it."

"What are you guy's talking about?" Doolittle asked.

"He didn't tell his old lady he got shot up north," Buster said.

The agent's mouth made a little round 'O', and he shook his head. "Oooh, that's not good. You have my sympathy."

I had a feeling that sympathy wasn't going to be the first reaction to my news.

Charles Ray

Chapter
Thirty-Nine

I immediately changed as soon as I got back home. I opted for a pair of cutoff jeans, short enough that the bandage on my thigh was visible, and an old Dallas Cowboys sweatshirt that I'd cut the sleeves off of. I knew Sandra would notice the bandage right away, but hoped she'd be at least a bit distracted by the shirt. She and I had the occasional discussions about my obsession with the Cowboys, a team that I'd been a fan of since my teens. Despite their five Super Bowl Wins, since 1998 they'd been on a losing streak, ending the 2002 season in fourth place in their league with a 5-11 record. They'd been going downhill ever since the owner hired Dave Campo as head coach, but my hope was with Campo's departure at the end of the 2002 season, things would turn around. Sandra wasn't much of a football fan, but when I first met her, she had, like most residents of the DC area, been a fan of the Washington Redskins, a team that I couldn't root for because of their name. I'd finally convinced her that rooting for a team with such a racially insensitive name was just wrong, but she hadn't come over to my side. She still didn't like America's team.

I considered having a beer while I waited for her to get home from school, but discarded that as a bad idea. She would be upset, and having me blowing booze fumes in her face wouldn't help matters. Instead, I made myself a pitcher of tea, filled a glass with ice cubes, and sat on the sofa listening to classical music on NPR and waited.

It was just after five when the front door opened and she entered.

I felt that tug of desire as soon as I saw her. Even a bit bedraggled after a day of jousting with rambunctious inner city high school students, she's the most beautiful woman I've ever seen. A lock of her blonde hair had escaped her careful attempt to arrange it neatly and hung over her left eye.

She stopped just inside the door. When she saw me, she smiled and her eyes lit up. Then, she saw the bandage, half of which was below the ragged edge of the leg of my shorts, and the light went out of her eyes. Her smile was replaced by a look of concern.

"What happened to your leg, babe?"

"I had a little accident," I said. I stood and crossed the room. I put my arms around her and pulled her in tight against my chest. "I missed you all weekend."

She rested her head against my shoulder for a few seconds. Then, she pulled back and looked me in the eyes.

"I missed you too. Why didn't you call before this morning?"

"After I called you from the hotel where I spent the night, I was in an area that had no cell coverage. It wasn't until this morning that my phone worked."

She was still eying the bandage.

"How did you hurt your leg?"

With some people you have to sugar coat bad news, but Sandra works in a school with kids who've seen drive-by shootings, drug deals going down in their playgrounds, and hookers plying their trade on the street corners down from their homes. In other words, with her, you just tell it straight.

"I zigged when I should have zagged, and the guy shooting at me got lucky," I said.

The only sign of emotion was a slight

widening of her eyes.

"You were supposed to pick up a painting, how did you end up in a shootout?"

I gave her the brief version of what had happened and why, ending with my little encounter with Richter and Kolchak. "So," I said at the end. "As you can see, it all ended rather well. The bad guys are either dead or in jail."

She poked a finger in my chest. "Do you ever have normal cases?"

"Sometimes." I shrugged.

"How did you allow yourself to get sucked into this mess? Where's that famous intuition of yours, that nose for sniffing out bad situations?"

"Yeah, it sort of let me down this time— almost. I was so focused on what was wrong about Richter I didn't even think to worry about the guys at the other end of the deal."

"I knew something was wrong when I talked to you on the phone this morning," she said. "I never thought it was this bad, though."

"It could have been worse."

"You got shot! Other than being dead, what's worse than that?"

She made a growling sound and pounded my shoulder with her fist. "Al Pennyback, you're giving me gray hairs. You were shot in the leg, and you wait until now to tell me about it? How could you?"

I cupped her chin and tilted her head so

that I could look directly into her eyes. She's only an inch shorter than me, so I didn't have to tilt it far.

"Look, babe, I didn't want you to worry, and I know if I'd told you on the phone that I'd been shot, you'd have worried yourself silly, wondering if it was worse than I said. This way you can see for yourself that it's just a minor wound."

She gazed into my eyes. It felt as if she was seeing into my soul. Her body was a bit stiff, but slowly it relaxed and she leaned into me.

We'd been through some tough times, the two of us. Once, she'd been kidnapped by a bunch of militia nutcases, purely by happenstance. They were actually after Buster's wife as a way to put pressure on him, and Sandra happened to be with her. I'd shocked her a bit with what I did to them when I rescued her and Alma, but she understood why I had to do it. In many ways she was like me. You don't mess with family or friends, not if you want to stay healthy.

She had been right about one thing, though. I hadn't been paying attention. When I first learned that my client wasn't what he claimed to be, I should have been wary of the whole deal. I should have done recon of the area, and research on the contact. I hadn't, and I'd had to navigate by dead reckoning to get out of a real sticky situation. Not the best way to run an operation. I wouldn't make that mistake again. There's a saying, 'that

which does not kill you makes you stronger.'
I don't know if that's true, but I do know that
the things that come close to killing you
make you smarter. If you burn a finger on the
stove, you know better than to put your
whole body against it.

I'd dodged a bullet—well, except for the
lucky shot to my left thigh—on this one. But,
I was back home now, holding the woman
who meant more to me than anything. In the
end, that's the only thing that mattered.

She looked up at me again, and laid a soft,
warm hand on my cheek.

"You know I love you, babe, don't you?"
she asked.

Yeah, I knew that. She showed it in a
thousand little ways, but mainly she showed
it by sticking with me, when most women
would have headed for the hills long ago. I
hadn't had a plan when I found her. I'd just
gone with the flow. Sometimes dead
reckoning's not a bad way to navigate.

"Yeah, babe," I said. "And, I love you too."

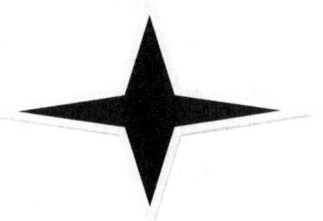

Chapter
Forty

On Tuesday, Sandra called her school and took a day off due to illness. She didn't tell them it was me, nor her who was sick, although I resented being thought of as sick. It didn't make a dent in her resolve, though. She drove me to the Army's Walter Reed Hospital on Georgia Avenue in upper northwest DC, and insisted on sitting in the room while a young captain who looked barely old enough to shave removed the bandages the EMT in Garrett County had put on and examined my wound. He made 'hm' sounds as he poked and prodded, but finally pronounced my injury as 'healing nicely,' and informed me how lucky I was that it had missed the femoral artery, hadn't hit a bone, and had only done minimal damage to muscle and tissue. After swabbing it with a red antiseptic and putting on a new bandage, he gave me a couple of shots to prevent infection. I didn't want the shots, but he was insistent, and the stern look on Sandra's face wore me down, so I sat there with a frown on my face while he jabbed needles in me. The little whippersnapper even had the nerve to pat me on the shoulder afterwards and congratulate me on not flinching when he stuck me. What I wanted to do was jab his needles up his ass, but that might lose me some of my retirement benefits, so I refrained. Before we left the hospital, the doctor strongly suggested that I stay off the leg for a few days to give it time to heal. Sandra assured him that I would do just that.

Then, she and Heather conspired to force me to stay home for a week. Sandra took Wednesday off, which gave validity to her 'sick' claim to her boss at school, and Heather took the day shift from Thursday, driving out to the farmhouse with her laptop and setting up shop in my living room.

In the meantime, by Friday evening, as Heather was packing her laptop and saying goodbye to Sandra who had just come home from school, I was getting a major case of cabin fever and was cranky with both of them. They both agreed that it might be okay for me to go to work on Monday, so I promised not to be cranky anymore. I wouldn't admit it to either of them, but the rest had done me good. My leg was still sore, but I was no longer limping. Looking forward to getting out of the house again, my mood was considerably better as well.

Neither Sandra nor I have a newspaper subscription. We get our news at home by listening to 'All Things Considered,' a news show on NPR. At the office, I get bits off the Internet, and Sandra gets the gossip from her students and fellow teachers.

On Saturday morning, after breakfast—Sandra still wouldn't let me run or work out—we were sitting in the living room listening to the radio, when I heard the first news about my little 'adventure.'

It started with the anchor saying that the FBI had announced the arrest of a noted international art thief, and gave Richter's name and the Boulware alias. He went on to say that, acting on a tip from a reliable source—yours truly—the FBI had raided Richter's residence in Potomac, Maryland, where they arrested him and a Russian associate whose name was not given. A search of the place revealed over a hundred stolen works of art, and a safe containing over a million dollars in cash. He prattled on for several more minutes, mostly about the negotiations between the U.S. State Department and several European countries who were screaming for Richter's extradition. The Justice Department was insisting that he be tried first in the U.S., mostly, I thought, out of embarrassment that he'd been able to circumvent border controls and surveillance for so long, but the Europeans were putting on a full court press, claiming that his most serious crimes had been committed on their soil. Of course, there was also a food fight going on among the Europeans over which country would get Richter first, but it was looking like Germany, being the country of his birth, was the big dog in that fight.

The only mention of events in Garrett County came at the end of the broadcast, a sort of throwaway piece about local police raiding a militia compound and shutting down a gun smuggling ring.

There was no mention of me in either story, which was fine with me. This might come as a surprise, but I really don't like the publicity. Oh, I know, and Heather has told me often enough, publicity means clients, and clients mean increased income. But, I just have this feeling about this line of work. Like they do with lawyers, people come to private investigators when they're in trouble. Somehow, advertising just strikes me as wrong. It's probably dumb of me. After all, how are people supposed to find you when they need you if you don't advertise? It's an issue that I'll never resolve.

When the news ended, a program of big band music from the 40s started. Neither of us was in the mood, so I switched the radio off.

"So, what do we do this weekend?" Sandra asked.

I ran my fingers lightly over her arm, causing the little hairs to stand on end and her to shiver.

"Well, I can't run or work out on the heavy bag, but I'm going crazy just sitting around doing nothing but listening to the radio. I need some exercise."

She looked at my fingers resting on her arm, and then looked me in the eyes.

"If you're thinking what I think you're thinking, is that really a good idea? It could cause your stitches to pull out."

"If I put too much stress on them, you're right," I said. "But, I was thinking of a way that wouldn't put stress on them at all."

It took a few seconds for her to process what I was getting at, but when she did, her eyes lit up and her cheeks turned red.

"Why, I do believe you're correct. That wouldn't put any strain on your leg at all."

She stood up, pulling me up with her.

It was no strain at all.

Charles Ray

Other books by this author:

Al Pennyback mysteries

Color Me Dead
Memorial to the Dead
Deadline
Dead, White, and Blue
A Good Day to Die
The Day the Music Died
Die, Sinner
Deadly Intentions
Death by Design
Till Death Do Us Part
Deadly Dose
Dead Man's Cove
Dead Men Don't Answer
Deadly Paradise
Kiss of Death
Death in White Satin
Death and Taxis
Deadbeat
A Deadly Wind Blows
Death Wish
Deadly Vendetta
A Time to Kill, A Time to Die
Dead Ringer
Dead Reckoning

The Buffalo Soldier series:
Buffalo Soldier: Trial by Fire
Buffalo Soldier: Homecoming
Buffalo Soldier: Incident at Cactus Junction
Buffalo Soldier: Peacekeepers
Buffalo Soldier: Renegade
Buffalo Soldier: Escort Duty
Buffalo Soldier: Battle at Dead Man's Gulch
Buffalo Soldier: Yosemite
Buffalo Soldier: Comanchero
Buffalo Soldier: Range War
Buffalo Soldier: Mob Justice
Buffalo Soldier: Chasing Ghosts
Buffalo Soldier: The Piano

Ed Lazenby mysteries
Butterfly Effect
Coriolis Effect

Other fiction
Angel on His Shoulder
She's No Angel
Child of the Flame
Pip's Revenge
Wallace in Underland
Further Adventures of Wallace in Underland
Dead Letter and Other Tales
The White Dragons
The Dragon's Lair
Dragon Slayer

The Last Gunfighters
The Culling
Frontier Justice: Bass Reeves, Deputy
  U.S. Marshal
Angel on His Shoulder-Revised Edition
Battle at the Galactic Junkyard
Mountain Man
Devil's Lake

Nonfiction
Things I Learned from My Grandmother About
  Leadership and Life
Taking Charge: Effective Leadership for the
  Twenty-first Century
Grab the Brass ring
African Places: A Photographic Journey
  Through Zimbabwe and southern Africa
A Portrait of Africa
There's Always a Plan B
In the Line of Fire: American Diplomats in
  the Trenches
Advice for the Insecure Writer
Looking at Life Through My Lens

Children's books
The Yak and the Yeti
Samantha and the Bully
Molly Learns to Share
Where is Teddy?
Catie and Mister Hop-Hop

Charles Ray

About the Author

Charles Ray has been writing fiction since his teens. He won a Sunday school magazine writing contest when he was thirteen, and having his byline on a short story published in a national publication forever hooked him on writing. During his time in the army (1962-1982) he often moonlighted as a newspaper or magazine journalist, and was the editorial cartoonist for the Spring Lake (NC) News, a weekly newspaper, during the 1970s. In addition to his writing, he was an artist/cartoonist and photographer for a number of publications, including Ebony, Eagle and Swan, and Essence, and had a monthly cartoon feature and did several covers for Buffalo, a now-defunct magazine that was dedicated to showcasing the contributions of African-Americans to the country's military history.

After retiring from the army, he joined the U.S. Foreign Service, and served as a diplomat in posts in Asia and Africa until his retirement in 2012. He has worked and traveled throughout the world (Antarctica is the only continent he hasn't visited), and now, as a full time writer, continues to globetrot looking for interesting things to write about, draw, or take pictures of.

A native of Texas, he now calls Maryland

home. For more on his writing and other projects, check one of the following Web sites:

http://charlesaray.blogspot.com
http://charlieray45.wordpress.com
http://www.twitter.com/charlieray45
http://www.facebook.com/charlieray45
http://www.flickr.com/photos/charlesray45/
http://www.viewbug.com/member/charlesray

Author's photograph by Denise Ray-Wickersham

www.ingramcontent.com/pod-product-compliance
Lightning Source LLC
Chambersburg PA
CBHW061957170626
46813CB00006B/2667